What the critics are saying…

"The love, passion and respect these two characters have for each other is obvious and lovely to see." ~ *Carolyn from A Romance Review*

"This one will have me rereading it often in the future." ~ *Lisa Wine from The Romance Studio*

"The love scenes are hot and heavy and all the characters are strong willed and realistic. It doesn't take long for the reader to know that Terra and Inez are made for each other." ~ *Patricia McGrew from Sensual Romance Reviews*

"Dream Stallion" will appeal to fantasy erotic romance readers. I certainly recommend it and I look forward to the next book in what promises to be a fascinating series." ~ *Mireya Orsini from Just Erotic Romance Reviews*

kate hill

DREAM STALLION

ELLORA'S CAVE
ROMANTICA PUBLISHING

An Ellora's Cave Romantica Publication

www.ellorascave.com

Horsemen: Dream Stallion

Electronic book Publication: October, 2003
Trade paperback Publication: May, 2005

Excerpt from *Horsemen: Captive Stallion*
Copyright © Kate Hill, 2004

Warning:

The following material contains graphic sexual content meant for mature readers. *Dream Stallion* has been rated *E-rotic* by a minimum of three independent reviewers.

Ellora's Cave Publishing offers three levels of Romantica™ reading entertainment: S (S-ensuous), E (E-rotic), and X (X-treme).

S-*ensuous* love scenes are explicit and leave nothing to the imagination.

E-*rotic* love scenes are explicit, leave nothing to the imagination, and are high in volume per the overall word count. In addition, some E-rated titles might contain fantasy material that some readers find objectionable, such as bondage, submission, same sex encounters, forced seductions, etc. E-rated titles are the most graphic titles we carry; it is common, for instance, for an author to use words such as "fucking", "cock", "pussy", etc., within their work of literature.

X-*treme* titles differ from E-rated titles only in plot premise and storyline execution. Unlike E-rated titles, stories designated with the letter X tend to contain controversial subject matter not for the faint of heart.

Also by Kate Hill:

Dream Stallion
Horsemen

Chapter One
Fighting Carriers

Terra's wings pounded, fighting the wind tearing across the clear morning sky. His equine legs galloped over air and his bent arms moved rhythmically for added power. Even after so many journeys, fast and challenging flights still thrilled him. His heart pounded in his man-torso, pumping blood through his magnificent Horseman body as he turned in mid-flight to face his students.

"Linn, tuck that chin before your neck snaps!" Terra bellowed.

The younger Horseman alongside him did as ordered, his chin falling to his chest, though his eyes remained fixed ahead.

Their wings beating around him, Terra led his troop on the downward slant toward the Running Way in the field two miles south of the training hall. Wind cut his narrowed eyes and fanned his heated body as he sped to his landing, ensuring that he beat his trainees. He wanted to check their landings after their long flight against the wind. Two days ago, they had passed their test and become Fighting Carriers. Today was the last time they would be together as a troop, for their assignments had arrived that morning and they would truly begin their careers.

Terra felt pride in his trainees though Linn, the boy he'd shouted to moments ago, was a particular favorite. Not that he could admit any favoritism. Fairness and toughness were qualities that had made him a most respected instructor for the past ten years. Unfortunately, he didn't train as often as his superiors would have liked. With all the time spent heading missions to the Spikelands, he wasn't always available for new recruits.

He grinned, remembering the reaction of General Sota when Terra had finally announced his recent decision. That had been two weeks ago, long enough for him to see these recruits through their test and give himself some extra time to consider what he truly wanted. The two weeks had proved as marvelously agonizing as the past several months. She still visited his dreams every night. They'd spoken, kissed and hovered on the verge of the most wonderful sexual experience he could ever imagine. She always pulled away, however, as if she could stop fate from binding them together tighter than chains forged by the Iron God himself. She, with smooth brown skin, raven hair and black eyes that reached into his soul, had stirred his desire and claimed his heart.

It had taken him months to find her, and when he'd arrived at her village, she'd been away on a mission. She was a Gatherer, of all things. Could a woman be any more perfect for him? A Gatherer fully understood his kind. They were Horsemen's respected partners. Terra imagined how much they could share, both privately and professionally. They could work each mission together. Already he could feel her on his back and imagine the sensation of her hands on his body—no matter what its form.

"Excellent!" Terra shouted to the first Horseman— Toni, a lean blond with a pale coat—as he floated to a perfect landing. The youth left the Running Way at a walk, his chest heaving from exertion.

Terra's own pulse raced, but he was accustomed to long, rough flights and wasn't yet close to his limit. In time, the recruits would toughen even more than they had over the past year of training.

"Very good!" Terra called as Linn dropped to the packed dirt clearing, his long blond hair and buckskin coat damp with sweat. The youth jogged after Toni.

Most of the others made passable landings. A few still needed improvement, though they'd all managed decent landings during their test. Kraig, a muscular, red-haired recruit, dipped precariously, his path unsteady.

"Pull up!" Terra commanded. At the last second, the youth did as he was told and managed a safer landing.

His jaw taut, Terra cantered to the red-haired recruit and ordered him to halt.

"Yes, Sir!" the youth panted.

"Back to lesson number one of flight. Takeoffs and landings are most important and should be executed with the utmost skill and precision!"

"Yes, Sir!"

"A landing like you just performed might get you or your Gatherer killed!"

"It won't happen again, Sir!"

Terra motioned for the other Horsemen to gather around him, standing at attention. He lowered his voice to a normal tone as he explained, "Landings are usually most difficult, particularly after a long flight. No matter how tired you are, strive for a perfect landing. It will save you pain and grief. There may be a time — though I hope to the Gods you never see it — when you've traveled so fast and long that you try to land properly but can't. When that happens, I guarantee you will be injured. Since there is no way you'll come out of it unscathed, the best you can hope for is that the injuries stay with you even when you change to Huform. The worst is that you die or kill your Gatherer."

"Understood, Sir!" the recruits stated together.

"Make sure you cool down properly. Dismissed."

Terra turned, trotted off the Running Way, and headed for the eastern meadows. His recruits would walk the training fields and swim in the lake, but Terra needed time alone. Filled with anticipation, he knew only the freedom of another long, fast journey could soothe him enough to sleep that night.

Once outside the training field, his speed increased to a gallop, his wings pressed tightly to his sides as his four long legs swallowed the ground. The scent of wildflowers and damp earth filled the air as he soared over the remains of an old rock wall, his hooves striking ground on the opposite side.

He imagined what it would feel like with *her* on his back, no saddle or clothing between them. Then he imagined claiming *her* in Huform, when his cock was most sensitive and ready for mating—and he would know four legs only with his two entwined with hers.

Spreading his wings and leaping, Terra rose high, overlooking fields, forests and rivers. His massive wings pounded the air then extended to their full width as he soared.

Terra drew deep breaths as he beat his wings, rising higher and forcing himself to greater speed. The woman filled his thoughts and his heart. He never imagined wanting anything as much as he wanted her. His desire was almost a physical need, winding inside him and twisting around his powerful Horseman heart. Did she feel the same as he? If so, their union would be easier than he hoped. If her passion was as strong as his, there was no way she could deny him.

Terra swooped toward the ground, his heart pounding as he slowed for a solid landing by the lake a mile behind the Training Hall. He walked along the water's edge as his breathing returned to normal. Terra glanced at his reflection in the water. His man-build was a powerful, broad-shouldered torso. His muscular chest was on the thick side, allowing room for a larger heart and more powerful lungs than a human man. Even in Huform, he was taller and bigger than most humans and a good many Horsemen. With a square jaw, skin turned golden by the sun and curly black hair that hung to his elbows, Terra thought he wasn't a bad-looking Horseman at all. His features were a little on the rough side, but some women liked that, and she had already seen him in their shared dreams. His appearance seemed to please her then.

Breaking a branch off a nearby tree, Terra waded into the lake and scrubbed his back, flanks and withers. Proper care of the skin and muscles was more important to shapechanging than most people realized. Poor maintenance after heavy exertion could cause all kinds of problems, such as skin disorders and muscle pain after shifting. Of course, it felt best for someone else to provide the massage, but Terra wasn't in the mood for company at the moment. When he finished with his beast half, Terra scrubbed and kneaded his torso and washed his hair. He squeezed moisture from the curly mass and stepped out of the water, shaking himself off before walking back to the Training Hall, where he brushed his coat and shifted to Huform before making his way to the great hall. His human legs felt strange after spending so much time with his beast-half. Still, they were very long, muscular legs. She had seemed fascinated by them in their shared dreams. What would she think of them in person? To hell with his legs, what would she think of *him* as a person?

"Terra." A Captain nodded to him as they passed one another in the corridor. Both were naked, but neither seemed to care. Nudity was common among Horsemen. After all, they couldn't shift shape with their clothes on. Modesty was a human issue. Still, Horsemen had taken to wearing clothing both for protection from the elements while in Huform and as a gesture of friendship toward humans. It had been that way for as long as anyone could remember.

Only the human females didn't seem to mind if Horsemen wore clothes or not. The females were more likeable than the males, anyway. And so necessary to both species. There were no female Horsemen. All were born male, and a human female had mothered each of them.

It was a great thing, to create a child with a female, and it happened far less often than when humans mated with their own kind.

Terra didn't doubt that he and his woman would create children, however. Most couples who met through shared dreams became parents. Perhaps it was nature's way of uniting those who could procreate so the noble race of Horsemen would live on.

In the great hall, Terra sat down to a meal of fragrant stew, bread and a hearty salad of mixed grasses. General Sota joined him, and as Terra stood out of respect, the General waved him back into his seat.

"I just wanted to make sure you really want to go tomorrow," the tall, gray-haired warrior said, a knowing gleam in his eyes.

"Without doubt, Sir."

"I can't say I blame you. The lure of a woman is powerful, particularly if it's a dream match."

Terra nodded. There was no way he could admit before his superior just how powerful his need for her was.

"I'm sorry you'll be spending most of your time away now, but at least we'll get you back here for training once in a while."

"My loyalty is still with the Fighting Carriers, Sir. Where you need me, I will go, though I admit I'm grateful you've agreed to station me at her village of Hornview."

"No, Terra, your loyalty is with the woman. You know the legend. Once you take your dream woman, you place each other above all else. It's true, too. I've seen it happen."

Perhaps the General understood after all.

"Good luck, Terra." Sota placed a firm yet comforting hand on Terra's shoulder before walking away.

Luck. Would he really need luck when he already had fate?

* * * * *

"For the last time, I said no! I do not want to see him, meet him or talk to him!" Inez bellowed, jerking her thick black hair into a tail at her nape and securing it with a strip of leather.

"Inez, you're crazy!" Susana stared at her friend in wide-eyed disbelief. "This is your dream lover. Don't you understand that?"

"Yes. I understand. So we shared a few dreams. It doesn't mean we have to spend the rest of our lives together!"

"Excuse me, but I believe it does." Susana folded her arms beneath her ample bosom and tapped her foot on the shed floor.

Inez had banished herself to the shed that morning after her Carrier, a Horseman she had been stupid enough to call her best friend, had informed her he was pairing with another Gatherer. Why? Because the village Chieftain had told her a Horseman called Terra was arriving to claim her as his mate. The mention of the lover she met almost nightly in dreams had nearly turned her legs to water. She'd told herself they were normal dreams, though deep inside she'd felt a spark of magic in them. Of all the women in the world, why did she have to be among those bound to a frustrating, fascinating Horseman?

She knew their culture intimately. Ever since childhood, all she'd ever wanted to be was a Gatherer, to work alongside those magnificent beasts, seeking good lives for both of their peoples. They possessed unimaginable power, speed and stamina, far surpassing almost every other species in the world. Their man/beast bodies endured hours of top-speed running and flight while bearing the weight of riders and cargo. In spite of their superiority they were loyal, intelligent and usually decent. They were also arrogant, boastful, and whether they admitted it or not, looked down on humankind as a whole.

Inez loved them. She hated them. She admired them. But there was no way in hell she wanted to marry one.

"Just because we've shared a few dreams doesn't mean I have to jump when he snaps his fingers!" Inez roared, shoving her feet into her riding boots and heading for the door. "I'm going out. This Terror, uh...Terra better not be here when I get back!"

"He searched months for you. Surely you can at least say hello to him?" Susana pressed. "Inez, he's absolutely gorgeous!"

Inez knew that all too well, not only from her dreams, but because she'd seen him arrive. She'd been watching from behind a tapestry—a disgraceful position, but her curiosity had gotten the better of her. She had to see if he was as stunning in the flesh as he had been in her dreams. When he'd stepped into the longhouse to greet the Chieftain and seek her out, Inez had, for the first time in her life, felt giddy with desire for a man.

He was tall—so, so tall. And big. His long, lean legs, curved with muscle and encased in black trousers belted with a strip of leather, stood braced apart. Muscles rippled beneath the flowing black shirt he wore. The ties had been opened, revealing a good portion of his massive, hair-roughened chest. The tips of his pointed yet delicate ears poked through his long curly black hair, two braids dangling from his temples. Horsemen's ears had far more mobility than those of humans. They were able to express their emotions through ear movements, such as twitching forward when pleased or pinning close to their heads when angry or upset. While some women found this characteristic strange, Inez had always considered it endearing.

Terra's square jaw was smooth-shaven, not at all the Horsemen's style. She wondered if he'd shaved to meet her, since he'd been bearded in her dreams. His nose was well shaped, though on the large side, permissible for a Horseman. At the tremendous speeds they traveled, large noses, strong hearts and powerful lungs were mandatory to their very survival. The intensity of his enormous sea-blue eyes overshadowed his other features, however. Those eyes seemed to notice everything. Inez had actually trembled, fearing he'd seen her behind the tapestry. If he had, he gave no indication as he'd spoken to the Chieftain in a voice so deep and rumbling it was as if some great animal, such as a tiger or bull, had learned to speak in words.

Just thinking of him made Inez's legs shake, though she continued protesting, "I do not want to get married!"

"Why?" another deep voice asked from the doorway.

Inez glanced at the dark-haired Horseman with a sturdy, brown beast-body. Moor had been her Carrier for over ten years. He was dependable, caring, and, like all Horsemen, quite in love with himself.

"Because I don't!"

"You're a caring young woman and should marry," he continued.

Susana cast him an approving look. "He's right."

"I always said I would exercise my right of freedom as a Gatherer. Most women must marry, you know that, but Gatherers have the same privileges as freemen."

"What Terra offers is a rare thing," Moor said quietly.

"I know what he offers! He struts in here as if he's a Chieftain himself and demands my presence. To hell with him!"

Susana narrowed her eyes. "He demanded your presence?"

"He said he needed to meet her and wouldn't leave until he did," Moor said. "What he meant was, the dreams have made him desperate and his heart is yours."

Inez lifted her eyes skyward and snorted in disgust.

"You dare question the power of Horsemen's dreams?" Moor glared at her, his pointed ears sweeping close to his head as his temper reared. "And in my presence?"

Inez felt a twinge of guilt. "I'm sorry, Moor. I know how special your relationship was with Anita."

"Part of my soul died with that woman, but I wouldn't have traded a moment spent with her," he said. "If you give yourself a chance with Terra, you'll know a love as great as I did."

"I think I'm going now," Susana murmured, resting a hand on Moor's broad shoulder before leaving.

Inez wanted to leave as well, but knew Moor would follow her to make his point. She wished he'd leave her alone. Between her lust for Terra and the memories of true love gleaming in Moor's eyes, her resistance was shattering.

"Inez, you're a kind, decent woman and a great Gatherer. I love you as a daughter. Would I push you toward a man I didn't believe would care for you? I know of Terra. His reputation—"

"I know about his reputation. He's an elite Fighting Carrier. The biggest, fastest, and most cunning of his kind. In short, he's trouble."

"He is a man who has come to pledge his heart to you, who has left his own life to seek you out. Give him a chance, and he'll give you loyalty such as you've never known."

"But will he treat me as an equal?" She held Moor's gaze. "I've worked very hard as a Gatherer. I'm not going to become a housewife and—"

"If that's his intention, then why has he agreed to become your Carrier?"

"It's a ploy."

"No. Just a partnership. One he wants with you."

"But will he—"

"Only Terra can answer your questions." Moor's gaze intensified. "He's come to pledge his life to you, Inez, to protect you until his final breath, and you can stand here denying him?"

Inez tried to think of an answer. Tried to fall back on a simple "Yes!" It didn't work. Not when faced with Moor's powerful words, particularly when she knew they were true. She'd sensed so much from Terra in her dreams— arrogance, stubbornness, integrity, and affection. He wanted to love her, of that she was certain. Even worse, in spite of all her protests, she wanted to love him, too. What she feared was giving up her independence, her freedom of having no one to answer to, either family or husband.

However, with that freedom came great loneliness and an empty space Terra—beautiful, powerful Terra— could fill.

"All right," she sighed. "I'll meet him."

"Good. Come with me."

"You go. I'll be along."

"No, I don't trust you."

"I'd like to fix myself up a bit first."

"You look fine." Moor grasped her upper arm and dragged her toward the longhouse.

She jerked away, striding ahead, her chin lifted, her expression cool in spite of how she shook inside.

As she stepped into the longhouse, the villagers mingling and performing chores stared at her. She didn't pay attention to them, however. Her gaze fixed on Terra.

"Inez, this is Terra," began the gravel-voiced Chieftain seated at the head of the long wooden table.

"Yes. I know," she stated, extending her hand to the Horseman.

He grasped it. Inez tried to keep her stomach from tumbling. His touch was firm but gentle, his palm callused. Like most Horsemen, his body temperature was much higher than that of humans, and his warmth seemed to spread through her hand, up her arm and settle deep in her pussy. Damn, she was already wet for the man and he hadn't even spoken a word, merely held her hand and stared at her with those huge blue eyes.

His thumb stroked her knuckles. "I'm so pleased, Inez. It's taken us so long to meet—at least in the flesh."

In the flesh. Gods, she wanted his flesh in hers right now!

"I suppose it couldn't hurt us to say hello."

"I'm told you don't want me."

Inez glanced over her shoulder, wondering how many of the villagers were listening. They all pretended to work, but their ears tilted toward the scene being played at the head of the Chieftain's table.

"I haven't wanted a husband, that's true."

"No," he released her hand, his gaze fixed on hers, "I'm told you don't want me in particular. Why?"

Inez sighed, shaking her head. "Do you think we could talk about this in private?"

"It would be my preference. You're dressed to ride. I'll change form and meet you in your village's Running Way."

"I never said anything about riding you!"

Repressed giggles sounded throughout the room as maids and servant boys hid their grinning faces.

"Will you all be quiet and go about your work!" the Chieftain roared. "Inez's Horseman is none of your business!"

The chuckles ceased and the servants dispersed.

"I like the sound of that." Terra's full lips turned up in the slightest smile. "Inez's Horseman. See you on the Running Way."

Without another comment, he strode out of the longhouse.

Susana, who had been watching from a corner of the room, rushed to Inez. "Oh, you get to ride him! I saw him when he landed earlier, he's —"

"So did I," Inez snapped. She'd been spying then, too. His beast half was just as magnificent as his man half.

"The last thing I need right now is to ride him," Inez muttered as she made her way out of the hall, Susana at her heels. As lust-ridden as she felt, she doubted she could endure him between her legs without betraying herself. "I never should have agreed to meet him."

"He seems kind enough. And he's so attractive, Inez — for a man with primitive features, that is."

"Primitive? You mean masculine."

Susana grinned. "I meant no insult, but it's good to know you like him enough to defend him."

"I don't think an elite Fighting Carrier needs defending."

Inez walked to the Running Way in the field west of the longhouse. Several other Horsemen and a few Gatherers milled around, preparing for flight. Another building, nearly as large as the longhouse, stood a short distance from the Running Way. It was used to keep tack and for the Horsemen to shift shape in private.

Terra emerged from the building and Inez's knees weakened. Again. The man was turning her to pudding and she both loved and hated it. She'd just better make sure he didn't know how she felt about him.

"Oh, Inez," Susana breathed as Terra strode to the Running Way. His beast body was that of a tall, well-muscled stallion, far bigger than any Horseman in the village, even Moor. His short, gleaming coat was glossy black, save his four white feet. Large, black wings tipped with white sprouted just below his beast shoulders and pressed close to his sides. His tail was as long, full, and curly as the hair on his head that was now wound into a tight braid flat to his scalp and dangling down his back. Inez's heart pounded. He must be planning quite a flight to have bound his hair so. Most Horsemen braided their hair or wore it short to keep it from lashing their riders and flying in their own eyes during windy days or fast flights. The day was not windy—at least not down on the ground.

She noticed his man-half was bare, except for the thick leather harness wrapped around his shoulders and chest with two handles in the back for a rider to hold for balance. It was unheard of for a rider to cling to the torso of a Horseman while riding, just as it was a terrible breach of manners to stroke one as if he was a true horse. Asking permission to touch a Horseman was different. When approached nicely, most would consent to their beast back and flanks being caressed. They were beautiful creatures, and the desire to touch one overwhelmed most humans, especially when they first saw one up close.

At that moment, Inez had a mad passion to run her hands over Terra's glossy flanks.

"Would you look at him." Inez sounded bitter. "It's as if he knows he's the most beautiful thing anyone here has ever seen!"

"Have fun," Susana whispered with a giggle.

Inez fired a furious look at her friend before straightening her back and approaching Terra.

"I didn't adjust the stirrups. You can do what you like with them," Terra said, glancing at the saddle on his back.

"With your permission, I'll check the girth and mount," Inez said, using the proper etiquette for riding a Horseman.

"Please do." He offered her a sensual smile that she did her best to ignore.

She checked the girth on the saddle, noting he'd secured it perfectly. Her hands brushed his belly accidentally. His hair felt coarse but smooth against her knuckles.

"Would you move to the fence, please?" she asked. He was far too tall for her to mount from the ground.

He obliged. She swung onto his back and adjusted the stirrups, marveling at the heady feeling of sitting on him.

She'd learned to ride almost before learning to walk, first horses then Horsemen, but never had she experienced such a wave of giddy pleasure just from sitting astride a creature.

She fitted her hands into the grips, careful not to touch his skin. The muscles of his shoulders and back were incredibly well developed, as were his arms. She longed to see if they felt as hard as they looked and to feel the warmth of his skin, but she refrained from even suggesting it.

As he strode forward, he glanced at her over his shoulder and whispered, "When we get high, if you want to forget the grips and hold onto me, you can."

"Not necessary," she said, her jaw tight. "I'm a very good rider."

"Suit yourself." He wrinkled his nose and winked before turning his attention to the Running Way. He walked for several moments before moving to a trot, then a canter.

Inez tried to calm her excited breathing. He moved so perfectly beneath her, it was as if they were truly one creature, and not just because she'd learned to ride well. They were soul mates. She knew it. The dreams hadn't lied. The problem was, could she live with it?

Terra's massive wings lifted as he switched to a gallop. Inez's knees gripped the saddle and she leaned close to his back, shielding herself against the wind. His wings pounded the air as they soared. Inez could have laughed aloud. It was like riding a tornado, except she felt perfectly safe.

"All right?" he called.

"Yes! Fantastic, actually!"

"I aim to please!"

He tilted, soaring higher, then flattened himself out, beating his wings as his legs churned beneath her. As many times as she'd flown, she'd never gone so fast! Moor was an excellent flyer, but this was unprecedented! She could have gone on forever. She began to wonder if Terra could as well. He galloped on air, racing over fields and lakes. Villagers' huts were tiny dots below. The sun felt warm and the breeze pleasant, but nothing compared with the perfection of the magnificent Horseman beneath her.

"You ride well!" he called.

"On you it's simple!"

"I need to turn up fast. Mountain ahead! Hold on!"

He tilted so sharply that she flung her arms around him—at least she told herself it was due to the swiftness of his motion. In truth, she and Moor had gone through horrible storms and some pretty quick turns and she'd never clutched him as she clung to Terra now. Her arms wound beneath his and she clasped his chest to keep her balance. It was far better than the grips ever were! His entire torso felt like hot granite beneath smooth, slick skin, except for his chest which was matted with soft hair. She gripped the plates of muscle and pressed her cheek to his sweating back, closing her eyes and enjoying the sensations of the flight—and the man. His heart slammed against her palms pressing against his ribs as she gripped him tighter.

I'll never let you go, Terra! she thought, her breathing quickening, almost keeping time with his. *Never!*

His descent began, yet she still clung to him, her arms tight around his torso, her knees squeezing the saddle until her legs ached. Her pussy felt like hot liquid and it throbbed, as if approaching climax.

He landed so smoothly she might not have known had the wind not suddenly ceased and she could hear again. He continued at a walk, taking several deep breaths. She marveled at his stamina. She'd seen Horsemen panting after slower, shorter rides than they'd just completed.

Inez's legs relaxed, as did her arms, though she didn't release him. She stroked his hot, damp chest until his hands closed over hers.

"Inez." He glanced around at her.

She tugged her hands from his and dismounted, walking to his front, her body trembling from the deepest sexual desire she'd ever felt, yet it was more than that. Her belly quivered and her throat constricted. It was as if he'd forced his way into her soul. She knew from the expression in his eyes he felt the same.

"I came for you," he stated. "I want you."

"We don't even know each other."

"Then I'll stay until you feel you know me."

"Why didn't you keep away and leave it as a dream?" She folded her arms across her chest and turned away.

Suddenly she found herself in his embrace, lifted off the ground. She slipped an arm around his neck and placed her free hand on his chest. His blue eyes bore into hers and his lips parted slightly as he bent his head, covering her mouth with his. Inez's eyes slipped shut and her tongue joined his, tasting and stroking. His lips felt so soft and moist, his breath tasted of fresh spring herbs.

"We've shared dreams for months, Inez," he said against her lips, his deep voice rumbling in his chest. "We belong to each other. Tell me you'll give it a chance. Let me share your bed tonight, and if you find you don't want us to part, say you'll marry me in the morning."

"I always said I'd never marry."

"You want to stand on principle?"

"I don't know."

"Find out tonight. Give us that. After so much anticipation in dreams, I feel I'll go insane without you."

Inez couldn't control her smile.

He grinned. "Is that yes?"

"All right. Just tonight."

He nodded, kissing her again before placing her on her feet. "We'd better get back. A storm's coming."

"How is it you Horsemen can predict the weather?"

He shrugged. "It's a gift. Must be the beast in us."

With no fence to stand on, Inez allowed one of his thickly-muscled arms to assist her onto his back.

The ride home was just as fast and exciting. Inez thought at least one benefit of marrying him would be riding him outside as well as in the bedroom—if he turned out to be as good a lover as she hoped he would.

After landing on the Running Way, Inez dismounted.

"I'll meet you at the longhouse," Terra said, stroking her cheek with the back of his hand. "I need to cool down before shifting back to Huform."

"I'll walk with you," she offered.

He smiled. "Excellent."

A servant boy approached from the tack house and offered to take Terra's harness and saddle.

"Yes. Thank you," he said, removing his harness.

"I can take off the saddle," Inez said, "With your—"

"Inez, you don't need to constantly ask my permission. I'm not some sacred statue that can't be touched, and I don't offend easily."

Without another word, she unbuckled the girth. The boy took the saddle, blanket, and harness and headed toward the tack house.

Terra offered her his hand as they walked. "Tell me how you became a Gatherer."

"I love riding, and I wanted to do something to benefit my people."

"What about the freedom?"

"That's a benefit as well," she said. "How about you? Why did you become a Fighting Carrier when you could have taken a safer more profitable route, like the private Carriers?"

"Like you, I wanted to benefit my people. Without warriors, no mission would survive in the Spikelands."

"That's true enough."

He grinned. "And I like the excitement."

"Somehow I knew that."

They spent the next half hour walking and discussing their professions. Inez was glad to learn more about him, especially how he viewed missions. If they were to be partners, it was better to know now how each felt about—What was she thinking? She hadn't agreed to marry him—yet.

As they neared the village, the same boy approached Terra. "Would you like a rubdown, Sir?"

"I'll do it, Samuel," Inez told the boy.

"Of course, ma'am."

Terra raised an eyebrow, his ears twitching. "You will?"

"It's only good manners. I usually rub down Moor after he's been kind enough to act as my Carrier."

Terra's eyes fixed on hers, and she sensed a bit of disappointment. Leave it to an arrogant Horseman to think her offer of a rubdown was to flirt with him — even if that was part of her reason.

While Terra splashed himself with well water, Inez retrieved an herbal ointment, developed centuries ago by a Horseman healer, and slung a towel over her shoulder. Moments later, Terra stepped inside. She offered him some of the ointment which he rubbed into his chest, arms, and shoulders.

"It's decent of you to rub down your Carrier," he said. "Moor might miss you."

"Doesn't look like it," Inez muttered, nodding toward the far end of the house where Moor stood, a plump young servant massaging his man-torso while a slim brunette brushed his sleek brown beast-coat.

Inez's attention reverted to her own Horseman, her heartbeat quickening as she rubbed the ointment into her hands and began massaging his equine back and legs. With Moor, the rubdown had never been rushed, but it had been efficient. With Terra, she lingered, paying careful attention to each and every muscle and loving the smoothness of his sleek coat. She massaged the place where his wings joined his body, then moved lower.

"Gods, that feels good," he sighed as she kneaded one of his forelegs.

With hands still slick from ointment, she stood, facing him. Her palms splayed across his chest and her lips parted. She stood on tiptoe and he bent, his hands grasping her waist. Their lips nearly touched.

The Chieftain stepped into the tack house and asked, "Did you make a decision? It will be good having a Fighting Carrier around permanently."

"I'm not sure what I want to do yet," Inez stated.

The Chieftain looked irritated. "I thought you were discussing it?"

"We were."

"How was the ride?" Susana burst into the house, her gaze roaming from Terra to Inez's ointment-stained hands. "Good?"

"It was one of the best rides I've ever had," she replied. In truth it was the best, but since Moor might overhear, she didn't want to insult him.

"Wait until tonight," Terra whispered in her ear.

Inez tingled, but she refused to show it as she took a brush and ran it over Terra's coat.

Susana and the Chieftain left them alone.

"I'll change form and see you at the longhouse," Terra said, once the grooming was completed.

He winked as Inez glanced at him over her shoulder before she stepped outside.

Chapter Two
Dream Lovers

Before going to the longhouse, Inez stopped at the women's bathhouse built over a natural hot spring. There was another bathhouse for men, and some of the wealthier folk had private ones built near their homes. Inez saved some of the profit she made from every trip to the Spikelands and within the next couple of weeks would have enough for her own private bath. The idea of perhaps sharing the bath with Terra made her toes curl. It would be magnificent making love with him in the steamy water.

Hell, it would be magnificent making love with him anywhere, anytime, and tonight would be their first time together. *First.* Already she was thinking of the future with him. Resisting him in her dreams had been difficult, but now that she'd met him, it might prove impossible.

Susana and several village women glanced at her from the pool when she stepped into the bathhouse. Inez did her best to ignore their curious stares as she removed her travel-dirtied clothes and shook out her hair. She waded into the hot water and closed her eyes, allowing it to soothe her tense muscles.

"So tell me exactly what riding him was like," Susana said, excitement in her voice.

Inez opened her eyes and reached for a cake of soap resting by the edge of the pool. She rubbed the soap over her body and lathered her hair. "Honestly, Susana, you'd think this village has never seen a Horseman before."

"I've never seen one like *him* before," said one of the women—the wife of another Gatherer. "He's so big."

"And strong," giggled the local seamstress. "He gives new meaning to the word stallion."

"We have some handsome Horsemen in this village," Susana admitted, "but not like a Fighting Carrier. The only one up to par with him is Moor, and even he's not as big."

Or as fast, Inez admitted to herself.

"So tell us what riding him was like," Susana pressed.

Inez ducked under the water, rinsed off her hair, and stepped out of the pool. Wrapping herself in the robe she always stored in the bathhouse, she gathered her clothes. Before leaving, she glanced over her shoulder and said, "It was like riding a tornado—only hot."

"Hot," murmured the seamstress. "Horsemen do have that marvelous body heat. Inez, you're so lucky."

"Lucky. Either I become a wife or give up the man who's shared my dreams. If you ask me, the choice is damn lousy."

"Being married isn't so bad," sniffed the Gatherer's wife.

"I'm too used to my freedom," Inez told her.

"I thought he agreed to be your Carrier?" Susana said. "Your life won't change—except you'll have that virile, magnificent—"

Inez slammed the bathhouse door, unable to listen any longer to how wonderful Terra was.

Inez stalked out of the village and over the hill nearly a mile away to the cottage she'd built last year. Terra had said he'd meet her at the longhouse, but it would do him good to wait. At least he wouldn't get the idea she hung on his every word.

As Terra had predicted, rain began falling just as Inez opened her door. She glanced around the cottage's single large room. The shelves and table carried a layer of dust, and she'd tossed dirty clothing in a pile on the floor.

"Damn it," she muttered, lighting a fire and two lanterns before flying around the room in a cleaning frenzy. She ran a soft cloth over the dusty furniture, dumped the clothes in a basket and set it behind a painted wooden screen that had been a gift from Moor.

Folding her arms beneath her breasts, she looked around the room. At least now it was presentable. She sighed. Presentable wasn't enough. Inez removed every candle she owned from a wooden chest at the foot of her bed and placed them all over the room, covering the shelves and the fireplace. She chose a bottle of wine she'd been saving for a special occasion and placed it on the table along with two beautiful silver goblets her mother had left to her when she died.

Her pulse racing, Inez slipped the only dress she owned over her head. It wasn't a very nice dress, just a plain forest green tunic with purple flowers embroidered on the sleeves. The square neckline revealed a good deal of cleavage. Slipping her feet into soft green boots that matched the dress, she was about to walk to the longhouse when two sharp knocks sounded on her door.

"Who's there?"

"Terra."

Inez's belly fluttered as she opened the door and tilted her face upward, staring into his eyes. Back in Huform, he wore his black trousers and billowy black shirt that clung, drenched with rain, to his perfect body. Wet ebony curls hung loose down his back, save the two braids at his temples.

"Change your mind about our arrangement?" he asked.

"No."

"You changed your clothes, though." His approving gaze swept her. "You look beautiful."

Inez's lips tugged upward and she stepped aside, extending her hand. "Please come in."

He ducked his head to keep from striking it on the doorway as he stepped inside. His gaze covered the room. "You live alone?"

Inez slipped a knife from her boot—something she always carried for protection—and pressed it to his side, her other hand slipping around him and gripping his chest. "But I'm well able to take care of myself."

"I don't doubt that, Inez. Now do you plan to cut me or kiss me? The latter is much more appealing."

Inez lowered the blade, but before she could sheathe it, he grasped her wrist and jerked it from her hand.

"Don't ever pull a weapon on me again," he said.

Inez stared at him, feeling apprehensive for the first time since she'd met him. Had she been crazy inviting an oversized Horseman into her house and, even worse, promising to sleep with him? It didn't matter that, according to legends about shared dreams, they belonged together. What did she really know about him?

"You don't need to fear me, Inez. I'll never hurt you."

"My dagger?" Inez extended her hand, her gaze fixed on his. After a moment, he turned the blade and placed the handle in her palm. Instead of returning it to her boot, she rested it on the table.

His gaze followed her around the room as she lit all the candles and blew out the lanterns. Dozens of flickering lights danced in the dimness. She glanced at him, his face shadowed, though she still discerned his gleaming eyes.

"Would you like some wine?" she asked.

"No." His voice sounded hushed as he reached her in two long strides and placed his hands on her shoulders. Though his touch was gentle, the heat of his large hands seemed to encompass her entire body. "I want you, Inez. Give me what you've denied in dreams. Let me please you."

When he bent and kissed her, Inez wanted to protest, to tell him it was too sudden, but the words stuck in her throat. He was right. They'd tormented each other for months in dreams, stopping just short of fulfillment.

Terra's soft, moist lips parted against hers. His tongue slipped into her mouth and met hers with tender strokes that weakened her legs. Terra bent and grasped her buttocks, lifting her off the ground. Instinctively, Inez's arms clung to his neck and her legs locked around his waist. Even through their clothes the heat of his body soaked into hers. His muscles were rock-hard. His cock, pressing against her bottom, felt like a thick steel pike.

Her eyes closed, Inez angled her head to better explore his mouth. He kissed her upper lip then her bottom. Terra didn't seem to mind supporting her weight and he took his time kissing her, his lips and tongue learning every corner and crevice of her mouth and face. His hair felt so thick as she curled her fingers in it and massaged his nape.

Finally he walked to the bed and lowered her to it. Again he kissed her, then sat, gazing at her and stroking her cheek. When he stood to undress, Inez sat up and quickly tugged off her dress, wanting to watch him disrobe. His gaze devoured her nude body as he kicked off his boots and jerked down his trousers. The shirt was last to go. Inez stared at him, her mouth dry. His huge torso was as she'd remembered it from his equine form, the muscles chiseled and powerfully developed. His human legs were just as perfect — and the longest she'd ever seen. Hair dusted his thighs and calves of pale, chiseled granite. His feet were long and rather wide. Most fascinating of all was his cock. It jutted, thick and reddish, from a bed of kinky black hair. Heavy testicles dangled beneath like those of a prized stud. Horsemen were never circumcised, so his cock head poked through a heavy foreskin. Inez found the image both animalistic and arousing.

"You're so beautiful," he said, approaching the bed and stretching out beside her. One of his large, long-fingered hands rested on her hip, stroking gently.

"You must not like skinny women." Inez tried to sound teasing, though she meant her words. While not excessively fat, she had padding over muscles that were shapely from use. The life of a Gatherer required physical strength, both for riding and loading cargo. Though the Carriers performed the brunt of the work, Gatherers weren't just sacks of wheat plunked on their backs.

"You're rounded." His hand trailed over her ribs and cupped one of her full breasts. "I like that. Still, you're so small you hardly seem to weigh anything at all."

"Gatherers can't weigh too much or we're liable to kill you on journeys. I — "

Her next comment emerged as a gasp of pleasure as he took one of her nipples in his mouth. His tongue stroked the nub, the tip teasing it to alertness, the flat caressing it in moist, broad strokes. Those long fingertips sifted through the hair between her legs then one slipped into her pussy. She'd been wet for him since he'd stepped into the house and her desire was fast becoming a near-painful ache. Her clit throbbed even before he touched his wet fingertip to it and caressed in a gentle, circular motion. She writhed, closing her eyes.

Terra continued sucking and licking her nipple while his finger ran up and down her sensitive little nub. When he stroked the side of her clit ever so gently, it was enough to send her over the edge. She panted and pulsed while he sucked and rubbed, extending her orgasm.

Finally she lay still and satisfied, her heartbeat and breathing returning to normal. She opened her eyes and found him lying on his side, his head propped on his hand, staring down at her.

"I love watching you come," he said. "I've imagined giving you pleasure, watching you shake and writhe because of my touch."

"What about you?" She slid down the bed, closer to the erection pointing at her from below his muscle-ridged abdomen. Using one fingertip, she stroked him from base to head then curled her fist around him and slowly pumped the shaft.

His chest rumbled with a lustful sound as she used her hand to squeeze and stroke his cock. It grew even bigger, the ruddy head almost slipping from the foreskin.

"Push the skin down. Like this." He took her hand and curled his over it, showing her what he wanted. Inez gazed at the thick, smooth cock head with its fascinating little eye. Several veins riddled the shaft, a particularly distended purple one running along the underside.

Her stomach fluttering and heartbeat quickening, Inez pushed herself lower so her face was level with his cock. Extending her tongue, she gave in to the overwhelming desire to taste him.

Terra groaned and rolled onto his back. Inez followed, kneeling between his spread legs. She ran her tongue from the root of his cock to the head, pausing to explore the folds of his foreskin gathered at the base. The tip of her tongue tickled the underside and traced that prominent vein.

"Damn it, woman!" His voice sounded strained.

"Shall I stop?" She paused, glancing at him. His chest rose and fell with each deep breath. His half-closed eyes glistened with desire and he sipped air through parted lips.

"Not yet," he said. "I'll let you know when."

Inez lowered her head over his groin, her long hair falling across his abdomen as she clasped the base of his cock in one hand and licked it all over. Her free hand grasped his balls, though they were far too big for her to hold in one fist. As she lapped, she squeezed his sac. She took his cock head in her mouth and sucked, running her tongue over it at the same time.

"Inez, oh Gods!" he breathed, his hands grasping her head.

She closed her eyes as she lapped, sucked and squeezed, completely lost in his taste and in his delectable, musky scent. She wondered how much time had passed. Several of the village women often talked about their lovers and from what Inez had overheard, it usually took men little time to climax when stimulated in this fashion.

His cock was so big and hard, the skin stretched so tight, it looked and felt ready to burst. Terra murmured to her, some incoherent sounds of passion, but mostly endearments.

"Gods, woman, you have such sweet lips and tongue. Beautiful, beautiful Inez."

Pleasuring him had her so filled with desire that her pussy felt like a river of lava. Her clit tingled and her pussy lips ached. She wanted to feel him deep inside her. She wanted to cling to that powerful body as he claimed her.

"That's enough," he gasped, gently tugging her head from his cock. The taut muscles of his stomach and thighs clenched as he fought for control of his passion. He dragged her onto his chest, his heat permeating her skin. She kissed his neck, feeling his flesh pulse beneath her lips.

"Come here, Inez." He moved her onto her stomach and knelt behind her, snaking one arm around her waist and lifting her bottom. The position forced her to support herself with her forearms braced flat on the mattress.

He stroked her back with broad sweeps of his callused palms before grasping her hips and slipping his cock into her well-prepared pussy. Though he moved slowly, she gasped. His cock was so big and hard. It felt sooo good!

Inez closed her eyes as he pumped her from behind. He thrust long and slow, then increased to a medium pace that pushed her toward another climax. She wondered how long he could keep up the steady rhythm. Suddenly her orgasm forced all thoughts from her head except the intensity of the pleasure she felt, throbbing and shaking, as he continued thrusting.

She melted onto the bed. Her eyes refused to open, even as he turned her onto her back. He took one of her feet in his hands and massaged it. He kneaded her ankle and rubbed her leg from calf to thigh then began the same ministrations on the other leg.

"Rubdown feels good, doesn't it?" he asked, laughter in his voice.

Her eyes opened and she kicked him playfully. He caught her foot and kissed it.

Inez stared at his bulging cock. "But you still haven't—"

"The night has only just begun." He growled, a sound of deep desire, and grasped her legs, guiding her knees to a bent position and placing her feet flat against his chest. The mat of curling dark hair felt good against the soles of her feet, as did the steely plates of solid muscle. He edged closer, his cock sliding into her. The same steady rhythm began again and, as excitement grew, Inez rocked her hips. Her feet pressed against his chest and he used one of his hands to push them harder against him. She felt his chest rising and falling and noted through her half-hooded gaze that his eyes had slipped shut.

Orgasm built inside her, tightening her belly and throbbing in her clit and pussy. When she exploded, her heart pounding, she felt his thrusts increase and his breathing grow ragged, though he didn't come. As her orgasm waned, he drove her toward another before she had a chance to recuperate. Didn't the man ever lose control?

The last climax was slow in coming, but so intense she felt it from the roots of her hair to the tips of her toes. She lay, on the brink of sleep, as he slipped from her and lowered her legs to the bed.

He stretched out beside her and fondled one nipple then the other.

Opening an eye, she glanced at him. "Don't you ever get tired?"

"Takes much to wear out a Fighting Carrier, but I think I'm about ready." He kissed her.

Inez grasped the back of his neck and attempted to pull him to her for a kiss. She only succeeded in hauling herself upward instead. Either way his lips were hers. She licked his mouth and thrust her belly against his, trapping his engorged cock between them.

His eyes fixed on hers. "Before I do this, I have to know."

"Know?"

"Will you marry me tomorrow?"

Inez drew a deep breath. "How can we be sure?"

"If I can admit what's been in our hearts since we started dreaming of each other, why can't you?" Terra pushed her back into the mattress and covered her body with his. His cock brushed her hip and near-painful desire shone in his eyes. One of his arms supported his body weight as he loomed over her while his other hand cupped her face, his thumb tenderly stroking her lips. "I will not spill my seed in a woman who refuses to marry me. I never have, and I never will. I know once I flood your sweet, hot pussy with my essence, there could be a child, and I'll have no son or daughter of mine raised without the two of us mated forever."

Inez's heart pounded and her head reeled. Marry him?

"Tell me, Inez."

She shivered, locking her arms around his neck. "Yes, I'll marry you."

With a groan of utter passion, Terra thrust his steely cock deep inside her. This time there was an underlying frenzy to his rhythm. Inez clung to him, her eyes closed, as incredibly, another orgasm kindled inside her. She exploded, her pussy throbbing, her arms and legs aching as they tightened on him. Terra pounded into her, every muscle in his big body straining, his skin hot and damp, drenching her with his passion. His breath raw in her ear, he stiffened and jerked as he burst inside her, filling her womb with his essence.

Panting, he rolled onto his back and dragged her to his chest. She listened to his heartbeat slow beneath her cheek. As she drifted to sleep, her last thought was that tomorrow she would marry the man of her dreams—the most wonderful, sensual beast she'd ever hoped to love.

Chapter Three
Bareback

Inez awoke smiling, her body pressed to the warm length of Terra's. Her knee brushed his semi-erect cock, her foot resting against his hair-roughened leg.

"Good morning." His chest rumbled beneath her ear as he spoke. His fingers sifted through her hair and he tugged her a bit closer.

"I think it will be." She smiled, pressing a kiss to his chest. "I wanted to ask you what's probably a silly question."

"Ask."

"When you're in horse form, do you mind being stroked?"

Terra drew a deep breath, amusement and pleasure in his sultry gaze. "By you? I look forward to it."

"Do you want me to ask permission, as I would any other Horseman?"

"Tell me you won't stroke any Horseman but me." The humor faded from his expression, replaced by a possessive look that sent a shiver of desire from her head to her toes.

"I can't think of any reason why I'd want to—now that I have you."

Terra smiled, his arms tightening around her. He caressed her back with the flat of his hand. "You have my permission to stroke me at any time and in any form I'm in."

Inez dropped a kiss at the base of his throat before slipping from the bed. Combing her hair with her fingers, she reached for her robe and glanced at him.

He sprawled on his back, his big body appearing completely relaxed, though she knew by the gleam in his eyes he was fully awake and sharp. The sun was just rising outside, the soft light of dawn flowing through the window and brightening the room.

"I'm going for a swim in the lake," she said.

Terra stood, yawning and stretching his arms above his head, every well-defined muscle in his body tensing and relaxing. "I'll go with you. Then we can meet your Chieftain in the longhouse. He agreed to perform the marriage ceremony."

Irritation burned in her breast. "You didn't even know what my answer would be until last night."

Terra smiled, reaching her in two strides and hauling her to his chest. "I knew."

"You're an arrogant son-of-a-bitch."

"I've been called worse." He released her, playfully slapping her rump. "Let's get washed then married. Afterward I'll take you for a ride."

Inez took a couple of towels and headed for the door. He caught her arm and kissed her forehead. "Don't be angry."

"Why shouldn't I? You took much for granted."

"It was just common sense. If you loved me even a bit as much as I love you, there was no way you'd refuse to marry me."

Inez shook her head, staring into his eyes. "You really believe we can fall in love through our dreams?"

"They weren't just any dreams. They were real—at least for us. You're the same woman I've desired and loved every night for what seems like forever. Am I any different than you remember from your dreams?"

Inez tried pulling away, but he refused to let her go. Finally she said, "You're the same. Confident. Arrogant. Beautiful."

"Thank you," he whispered before brushing a kiss across her lips.

Together they walked to the river running behind her house. They washed and dried off with the towels, then dressed and made their way to the longhouse. Terra kept his Huform. Inez gazed at him as they walked, hand in hand, across the meadow.

Villagers were already going about their work when they arrived at the longhouse. The Chieftain greeted them with a smile and opened his arms wide. "Congratulations! Come, and I'll get this ritual over with. It will be wonderful having you here, Terra. A Horseman of your size and strength will be a marvelous asset to our village."

"He's adding up the profits of future Gatherings," Inez whispered, unable to keep the sarcasm from her voice.

"It's only good business," Terra replied, squeezing her hand affectionately. "But I've gotten the better end of the bargain."

The ceremony took less than five minutes. Susana and several of the servants stood as witnesses. Afterward, there was a fine breakfast at the Chieftain's table.

In the middle of the meal, a clatter of hooves — small true-horse hooves — echoed outside. Moments later a tall, lithe blond man strode into the longhouse. Dressed in chainmail, he carried a helmet in one hand. A sword hung from a sheath on his hip, and his shrewd green gaze swept the room before fixing on Inez.

The blond warrior smiled and approached, nodding to the Chieftain and casting a curious glance at Terra before focusing his full attention on Inez.

"My dear," the blond said, his gaze fixed on her full breasts visible above the square neckline of her dress.

"Casper." Inez nodded, an uncomfortable feeling winding through her belly. Casper was Captain of the Chieftain's personal guard. Of course he had nothing to do with Gatherings. They were supervised by Horsemen Fighters, either private or by the Fighting Carriers. Casper tolerated the presence of Horsemen, admitted the necessity for them, but everyone knew he disliked their kind. About as much as Inez disliked him.

"Have you missed me while I've been away?" Casper leered at her.

"No." Inez glanced at Terra and saw the flames in his blue eyes. The sharp tips of his ears pressed so tightly to his head they disappeared in his curly black hair. His immediate dislike of Casper was almost tangible, and she knew she'd best make an introduction fast, before Casper continued with his usual disgusting flirtations. "Casper, I'd like you to meet my husband, Terra."

Casper's eyes widened a bit, then his lip curled. "This is the Horseman who claimed to share dreams with you? You actually *married* him?"

"And you are?" Terra stared hard at Casper.

"I'm the man she should have married." Casper knocked an empty glass over with a clang.

Terra stood, glaring down at the warrior. "You have a problem, boy?"

Casper's teeth ground, but he turned away from Terra and stared at Inez. "I've proposed to you dozens of times and you always said no. We were a perfect match, Inez, yet you marry this...*Horseman*!"

"Who I marry is not your concern, and if I were you, I'd mind my manners. I don't like the look in my husband's eyes right now, and while I could always defend against the likes of you, Terra is quite beyond my control."

"I'm not afraid of any Horseman!"

"Maybe you should be." Terra's quiet tone sounded threatening. "Boy."

Casper's face flushed with rage, but he nodded slowly. "I don't understand you, Inez. Why did you marry him but not me?"

"Because I'm not in love with you."

Casper glanced around the room, as if suddenly aware—or concerned—with the servants and villagers who'd gathered to watch the scene at the head of the Chieftain's table.

"All of you go about your business!" Casper bellowed, pointing at several of the onlookers. They dispersed, glancing over their shoulders as if wondering what more they could overhear. The blond warrior curled his lip at the newly married couple. "Then all I can offer you is congratulations—or perhaps condolences are more apt."

"Casper, don't be angry about this marriage," the Chieftain said. "There are other women for the taking who would love to marry you and bear your brats. Sit and eat. Refresh yourself after your journey."

"I'll be in the bathhouse." Casper bowed from the neck in the Chieftain's direction but glared at Terra and Inez before stomping off.

"I can see your distaste for marriage if that's the sort of proposals you've had," Terra stated, glancing at Inez as he took his seat.

"I'm sorry for Casper's attitude," the Chieftain said. "He was upset when Horsemen's law refused to allow human warriors to head the Gatherings. It only makes sense that Horsemen should be in charge, considering they're the ones powerful enough to make the journeys and defend against the creatures of the Spikelands."

"He's jealous of Horsemen," Inez said. "Always has been."

Terra's long fingers traced shapes on the side of his mug. Finally he stood, offering Inez his hand. "I'm eager to be alone with my new mate."

"I don't blame you." The Chieftain grinned. "But I trust you'll both be ready to join the Gathering Party on Friday?"

"We'll be there," Inez said, then glanced at Terra. "Providing you're up to it?"

"I'm looking forward to it."

The Chieftain smiled before Inez and Terra left the longhouse.

"I can hardly wait to get you back in bed," Inez admitted.

"Later. Right now I have a favor to ask you."

"What?"

Terra glanced around, as if to ensure no more of the villagers were eavesdropping. He bent and spoke close to her ear, his breath warm against her face and neck. "I want you to ride me again."

Excitement rippled through her. "I can hardly wait."

"Naked."

Her heart pounded and she stared up at him. A grin tugged at his lips and his eyes glowed with lust.

Naked. To ride his beautiful, sleek body, naked. To feel his glossy black coat against her bare flesh and feel his mighty muscles bunch and ripple between her legs...

"Naked?" she repeated.

"Hell, yes, woman." His hand gripped hers tighter, his eyes boring into hers. "Naked."

"I think I can oblige." She tried sounding nonchalant. Difficult when her entire body trembled with desire. He must have felt it, or was he trembling as well?

She stared at his tall, strong body and noticed a quickening of his breath. It made her feel powerful, that the thought of her riding him naked could speed the respiration of this creature who was built to run and fly many miles at blinding speeds.

"In the woods behind my cottage—"

"*Our* cottage."

"Our cottage," she smiled, "there's a favorite clearing of mine. We could go there and be alone. Then there are miles of open meadows that are almost always empty."

"Let's be on our way." He gazed at her. "I can scarcely wait, Inez, to feel your smooth, bare legs wrapped around me."

"Neither can I," she breathed.

They walked at a quick, steady pace to the woods. At least it was quick to Inez. With Terra's long strides, he probably felt as if they were creeping.

"It's a little further," Inez said as they picked their way along the winding, rock-strewn path.

As they walked, they cast each other lustful glances. Inez tried to control the racing of her heart and wished the wetness between her legs would go away. It would be embarrassing for her—and far too big a compliment for him—if she was already damp when she mounted him. In truth, she wished she could ride him and not reveal any sexual desire, though she knew it was impossible. Even with the saddle, she'd nearly climaxed during the last ride.

A brook ran through Inez's favorite clearing. Mossy rocks were scattered throughout the dirt semicircle and sunlight shone through spaces in the trees.

While Inez undressed, Terra disappeared into the trees. She knew he'd gone to change shape. It was proper etiquette for Horsemen to do their shifting in private, but she'd have to tell him not to bother next time. She wanted to see what it looked like. Common theory was humans would be disgusted, but Inez knew nothing about Terra would disgust her. Her feelings for him were too deep, though she wasn't yet ready to admit such surrender.

She waited, slightly chilled from the forest in spite of the warm day. Terra stepped into the clearing, his hair loose down his back, his beast half gleaming black, his wings folded tightly to his sides. He flicked his lovely tail and approached, holding out a piece of rope. "Once you're on my back, you can bind my hair."

She nodded, standing on a rock and swinging herself onto his back as he moved his wings to accommodate her. She resisted the urge to close her eyes against the marvelous sensation of his hard, hairy equine back against her flesh. Though she knew he must have felt her wetness, he refrained from making a comment, and for that she was grateful.

"I'm guessing you can ride bareback?"

"Of course."

"And if you want the truth, I like you to hold me instead of the harness."

"I like it better, too, even though we'll have to use the harness on Gatherings."

"Of course. Wouldn't want to cause a scandal." He winked at her over his shoulder.

Inez braided his hair and tied it with the rope. All the while he stood still, using his tail to flick the forest insects from them both. The gentle sweep of his curly tail against her bare back and shoulders was pleasant and might have been soothing had it not been for the barrage of sexual thrills attacking her entire body simply from the feel of him between her legs. Gods, when he moved, it was going to be so hard to keep from squirming!

"Ready?" he asked.

"Whenever you are."

She gripped with her knees as he lurched forward, his hooves striking the packed dirt. Since he wasn't moving fast, she rested her hands against his sides and enjoyed the scenery as he splashed across the brook and back into the forest, this time heading toward the empty fields she'd spoken of.

"What village were you born in?" she asked.

"Silver Cove about fifty miles south of here."

"Do your parents still live there?"

"They're dead."

"It's the same for me."

"Have you always lived in Hornview?"

"No. The village I grew up in has since been deserted, but I love it here."

"And you always wanted to be a Gatherer?"

"I like your kind."

He grinned at her over his shoulder. "I'm glad."

They talked of trivial matters until the forest thinned and opened into a vast field with hills in the distance.

"Want to run for a while?" he asked.

"I'd love it."

"Hang on!"

Her arms slipped around his torso, clutching his chest, her knees gripping his sides. She squinted against the rush of wind as he broke into a gallop. His powerful legs churned beneath her, and she felt the play of his muscles as he ran. The distant hills were upon them in moments, and his hooves flew over grass as he galloped up and down several of them before she even noticed his hot body getting hotter.

"Having fun?" he called, scarcely breathless. Already her breathing had increased and she wasn't even doing the work.

"Oh yes!"

"I'm going to take off in a minute!"

"Go ahead!" The sound of his pounding hooves and the whipping wind echoed in her ears as his speed increased, his long legs stretching, tearing up the ground. Suddenly they were flying. His great wings beat and his legs continued racing, propelling them across the sunny sky.

Inez closed her eyes, her cheek pressed to his back. His heart thundered against her face as he tested his speed. She thought he'd been fast yesterday, but if possible, he was even faster at that moment. The power in his body cried out to her. In the air, the ride was much smoother than when galloping over ground. Though Inez kept the tension in her legs to keep from slipping, she was able to relax a bit. Perhaps that was a mistake. The rhythm of his strides seemed to rip right through her pussy. That combined with the sensation of her arms wrapped around his man-torso was enough to push her stimulated body closer to orgasm.

He devoured miles of sky, his wings beating and his body surging onward. His speed increased until it finally leveled out. Still he continued racing for what seemed like forever, and she wondered how long he could hold such speed.

The feeling of riding the wind itself was incomparable. His body felt like an inferno, and it kept her warm even when up so high in cooler air. Inez's hands kneaded his damp, hair-matted chest. Her breasts pressed against his sweaty back, the nipples scraping his heated flesh. Her eyes narrowed and streaming tears from the cutting wind, she rose high on his withers and buried her face in his neck, pressing her lips to the pulsating column of muscle and straining tendons. Her clit pressed against his back, feeling every delightful pulsation of his body as he galloped over air. The sleek black hair of his beast body grew damp with sweat, his wetness mingling with her own.

In a sudden burst of energy that seemed to come from some reserve deep inside him, he sprang forward, every muscle in his body straining for that last bit of speed. She felt his heart slamming against her palms and through his back, pulsing beneath her cheek. Inez's fingers bit into his chest and her legs clamped him hard as she came, her pussy and clit throbbing along with the wild beating of his heart. She moaned and panted, unable to keep her silence in the face of such intense pleasure.

His pace slowed, and she heard his harsh breathing as he spread his wings flat and coasted on the wind. Inez relaxed against him, using only enough strength to keep her seat as he descended, landing in the meadow by the woods.

He walked for several moments as his breathing returned to normal. She pressed kisses to his slick back and stroked his ribs, feeling hot rivulets running over his skin. Turning slightly, she placed a hand on his sleek rump, noting the sweat rolling off his coat. Between the excitement of her climax and the immense heat generated by his body, she felt nearly as sweaty as he. Gripping his sides with her knees, she lifted herself slightly, so the breeze fanned his back and her buttocks.

"Would you like me to get off?" she asked.

"Only if you want to."

She guessed from his tone he liked her exactly where she was.

"I take it you enjoyed yourself?" He glanced at her over his shoulder, his eyes glistening with mischief.

She felt herself blushing. "You did this on purpose. 'Come, darling, I want you to ride me naked.' You're the worst kind of flirt!"

He laughed. "Want to go for a swim in the lake?"

"I thought you'd never ask."

By the time he reached the next field, both had begun cooling off. Still, the water felt good as he waded in with her still on his back. She slipped off him and swam, though her gaze continued returning to him. She swam to him and slipped her arms around his neck, surprised when his human legs entangled with hers.

"Changing without a rubdown isn't good for you, is it?" she asked.

He shrugged. "Once in while it doesn't hurt, as long as we take care of our skin and muscles as a general rule. I just can't wait until we get back to the house to make love with you. I want you right now."

"You certainly earned it." She smiled, rubbing her nose against his. "What do you want? Anything you ask, I'll give you."

"Mmm," he purred against her lips. "I love the sound of that."

She grasped his hand, tugging him toward the shore. "Come lie in the grass."

"I'm not in the mood for a nap." He pulled her to his chest and gently nibbled her ear.

"Lie on your back because I want to lick and suck your beautiful cock until you explode in my mouth."

His eyes closed and he drew a deep breath, a dreamy half-smile on his lips. "Woman, that sounds so damn good."

She slipped from his grasp and swam to shore, sprawling on the sun-warmed grass and patting the space beside her.

Terra emerged from the lake, water streaking his broad torso and rock-hard legs. He stretched out beside her, leaning back on his elbows, his eyes dark with passion as he watched her crawl between his spread legs and curl her fingers around his cock. She pumped it a few times, though he was already hard for her, and rolled down the foreskin. Clasping the base, she licked her lips and crouched lower. Her tongue ran up and down his length and swirled around the sensitive head. Terra's body tensed with pleasure and she sensed he was trying not to thrust his hips. She closed her eyes and tongued every inch of his cock three times over then blew soft puffs of air over the tip.

Terra fell back on the grass and grasped her head, holding her with subtle pressure when she imagined he must have wanted to practically snap her neck from the pleasure. Every now and then helpless moans escaped his throat. His breathing grew ragged when she took his cock head between her lips and sucked in a steady rhythm. As she sucked, her fingertips tickled the shaft. She used one hand to grip his balls while she continued her delicious torment.

"Gods, Inez," he breathed. "Oh...hell and damnation!"

She grinned around his cock then began sucking deeper.

"Inez, stop now or I *will* explode in your mouth!"

In response she patted his inner thigh then reached around with both hands and squeezed his buttocks as she sucked. He could no longer stop his hips from thrusting. She panicked a bit at first, almost afraid he'd ram his enormous cock too far into her mouth. She relaxed her jaw to accommodate him, all the while lapping his cock between sucking motions.

"Ah! Ah! Ahhh!" he cried out. His hips bucked and his body stiffened then she tasted his essence before his spasming cock flew out of her mouth. She clutched it, rubbing the shaft, wanting to give him pleasure as complete as he'd given her.

Then he lay still except for his heaving chest. His breathing returned to normal quite fast, though he kept his eyes closed for several moments, a smile on his lips.

"I, uh, take it you enjoyed yourself?" Inez grinned as she flung his own words back at him.

He chuckled, the sound echoing from deep in his chest. His eyes opened and he reached for her, tugging her close and giving her a smacking kiss. "Now who's the flirt?"

"Not me!"

"Oh no?" He tickled her and she squirmed, laughing.

"Stop it, Terra!" She giggled. "Please stop!"

He did as she asked, looming over her and stroking wisps of hair from her face. Inez stared into his enormous blue eyes and realized he was not the stranger she'd tried telling herself he was. She *did* know him and she was already accustomed to his touch and expressions. Their union was like a fantasy come true. How could she have possibly considered denying it?

"We should go back," he said. "We left our clothes in the woods."

"Yes, and there's bound to be a meeting tonight for the Gathering on Friday. Moor went on today's trip with his new Gatherer. Since Spike season is almost here, there have been Gathering Parties leaving almost every day. There will be plenty of work for us."

"I'd planned on it. General Sota told me it was good the two of us might marry. He needed to send a Fighting Carrier here until Spike Season, anyway."

"The journeys have been tough, but I have no doubts you're up to it."

"And you. I'm looking forward to us working together." He kissed her before standing and wading back into the lake. He swam out deeply and she strained to notice any sign of his shape-change. A single shudder ran through him and his eyes closed briefly. When he emerged, it was with his equine half.

Since there were no rocks or fences for her to stand on to mount, he gave her an arm up.

"Sometime may I watch you change shape?"

He glanced over his shoulder at her and wrinkled his nose. "You won't like it. It's not very attractive."

"I don't care." She shrugged. "We're not always going to be attractive. I hope what we share goes beyond that."

"That's what I love most about you, Inez. Your heart. And, yes, I believe what we have does go beyond the superficial."

"Besides, if you can accept my unattractive mouth, I can accept a little shape changing."

"What do you mean, your unattractive mouth?"

"It's big and my teeth protrude something awful. Don't tell me you haven't noticed."

"I've noticed, but the best parts of me love it, if you get what I mean." He wiggled his eyebrows at her and flicked his tail across her back.

Inez blushed at his implication. She hadn't thought about how well her large mouth and buckteeth would suit an oversized Horseman's cock. "I guess it's not so bad after all."

"You'll never hear a complaint out of me," he said before picking up his pace to a gallop and heading for the woods.

Chapter Four
Gathering Rock Blood

For as far back as anyone could remember, Horsemen and humans shared a unique relationship. Human women would bear the Horsemen children to keep their race alive, and Horsemen would carry humans on the perilous journeys to gather Rock Blood. Rock Blood was the only cure to a plague that often swept through the human colonies. Without the treatment of Rock Blood, most people died of the disease, but with Rock Blood, the Plague was as harmless as a cold. The amazing substance grew below ground. When fully matured, Rock Blood's soft flesh formed a hard outer crust, protecting the liquefied center. It was the liquid that, when ingested by those infected by the Plague, produced an almost instant cure.

Two variations of Rock Blood existed. Each seemed capable of growing only under severe weather conditions. Because of this, just two places in the world produced Rock Blood — a small group of tropical islands and a larger group of arctic islands known as the Spikelands. Both groups of islands were home to fierce animals that constantly attacked whenever a Gathering Party stopped for Rock Blood. Though warding off the beasts would have been difficult without the help of the Horsemen whose skill for fighting was nearly as great as their skill for flying, humans still would have persevered and fought for themselves. It was the oceans that indebted humans to

Horsemen, oceans filled with flesh-eating plants that wrapped around ships and swimmers, dragging them into the depths to be devoured. Even sharks stayed clear of certain oceans, knowing the plants would rip them to shreds.

Horsemen carried the human Gatherers and their cargo across miles of ocean, through bitter cold and intense heat. They fought and worked alongside the Gatherers, ensuring the humans got their supplies of Rock Blood.

Hornview was closer to the Spikelands than to the tropics. Since cold-climate Rock Blood seemed to have the most success in curing the Plague, the Rock Blood from the Spikelands was most coveted. Harvesting, however, only occurred during certain months of the year. Though frigid even in summertime, the winter season was intolerable for human and Horseman alike. The Spikes came in winter, massive clouds of frigid air that froze every living creature on the islands—except for the Ice Lizards. Spikes arrived in vast waves visible from the sky. They had claimed the lives of many Horsemen and Gatherers in the early years, before it was decided that absolutely no gathering would be allowed in the Spikelands during the wintertime.

Winter was fast approaching, so Inez and the other Gatherers and Carriers worked diligently, making as many journeys as possible to store up for the months during which the only Rock Blood available would be the fewer and weaker harvests from the tropics. Gathering Parties left daily, with the Horsemen and Gatherers taking rotations. The journeys were long and grueling, bad enough for the humans snug on their Carriers' backs, but extremely punishing for the Horsemen. They flew hundreds of miles in each direction with no resting place along the way. On the home trip, their saddlebags were loaded with Rock Blood—not a light substance. A dip too close to the ocean would mean certain death, for the flesh eating plants would devour both Horseman and rider. Only the strongest Horsemen with the best endurance became Carriers, either in private business or as part of the Horsemen's Fighting Carriers.

The average Horseman made no more than two trips a week. The most powerful ones made three to five trips a week, though most preferred having a much-needed day to rest in between. Inez and Moor had often made those extra trips, and though Moor was extremely powerful, there were times when the journeys told on him. Recently, her old Carrier had disclosed that Terra's reputation was well-known among Horsemen. As a top Fighting Carrier, he'd sometimes make several flights in a day.

Inez considered Moor's story as she approached the tack house just after dawn on Friday. This would be her first working ride with Terra and she was curious to see if, as his reputation claimed, his stamina did indeed match his tremendous speed.

Adjusting her thick woolen tunic and cloak, she stepped into the tack house. Her gaze fixed on Terra, who stood by a wooden trunk. He'd shifted into his beast shape, this time in his full-coat. To protect themselves against the frigid weather in the Spikelands, Horsemen produced at will a full-coat of hair over their human head, neck and torso, blending with their equine half. Inez had seen many Horsemen in their full-coats, but again she was struck by Terra's primal beauty. His facial features were exactly the same, as was the shape of his magnificent torso, but short, dense, gleaming black hair covered every bit of skin. A white blaze, reminding Inez of a streak of lightning, ran from his forehead down to the tip of his long, well-shaped nose. He smiled at her, his blue eyes gleaming and his white teeth glistening against his hair-darkened face.

"Just about ready?" she asked.

"Yes." He took the sticky leaf of a Darrion plant and placed it across his nose. Many Horsemen used the leaves to ensure their nasal passages remained clear during long or fast flights. Heavy labor with difficulty breathing could not only cause Horsemen to pass out and kill themselves and their riders, but could also prompt serious lung damage.

Inez had seen some very good Horsemen ruined due to overwork, either because they and their Gatherers were greedy and overloaded the saddle with the hope of selling extra Rock Blood for profit, or because of prolonged flights. When a Horseman landed bleeding from the nose or worse, coughing blood, he was removed from duty for several weeks. Some had done permanent damage and were unable to perform long, fast flights ever again. Such a fate was terrible for a Horseman, especially a young one. For creatures born to run and fly, a quiet life was pure torture.

Terra had already donned his harness and a sheath about his waist, the handle of his sword just visible above it. As a Fighting Carrier, he would lead the party and defend with the Horsemen delegated as protectors while other Horsemen assisted the Gatherers in collecting the Rock Blood. He reached into the trunk near his front hooves and removed a black blanket.

"I'll do it." Inez approached, taking the blanket and placing it on his back. He then took his work saddle, complete with built-in pouches for holding cargo, and positioned it over the blanket. Inez tightened the girth and checked one of the pouches for an extra cloak and blanket for Terra when he landed in the freezing Spikelands.

"I just need to fill this then I'm ready," he said, tapping the water pouch hanging from the front of his harness. Though he couldn't drink much while traveling, he needed to keep from dehydrating over the long journey. He laughed. "When I was a boy, my father told me 'never drink too much right after exercise.' One day after racing with my friends, we passed a lake in northern country and I figured my father didn't know what the hell he was talking about. After all, he was an old-timer. I drank like I'd never seen water and got such bad cramps that less than an hour later my friends were carrying me home. Looked like an ass."

Inez grinned. "I guess you learned the hard way that older is wiser."

He grunted in reply as she followed him out of the tack house and to the well. Inez noticed Casper also standing by the well, his sword at his hip, his tunic and face dirty from training.

As Terra began filling his water pouch, Casper sniffed the air, making a face. "I seem to smell a horse."

"And I smell a pig," Terra snarled, striding toward Casper. The blond warrior tried standing his ground, difficult with a Horseman plowing him across the village square.

"Are you assaulting the Captain of the Chieftain's guard?" Casper demanded, drawing his sword. Terra didn't so much as reach for his.

"Put the weapon away. I don't have time for stupidity." Terra took one last step forward. Casper edged back, tripped and landed with his backside in a true-horses' trough.

Several villagers who had witnessed the confrontation snickered. Casper growled and grasped his sword, racing at Terra who picked up a nearby pitchfork and blocked several blows before knocking the sword from Casper's hand.

"I said I don't want to fight you, boy," Terra sneered. "If we must live in the same village, we can at least ignore each other, if not be civil."

"Civil? How does a beast be civil?"

"Why don't you start acting like a guard instead of an embarrassment?" Inez bellowed at Casper as she handed Terra the water pouch she'd finished filling for him. "Some of us have work to do. Come, my love." Inez grasped Terra's forearm.

Casper seethed as he picked up his sword.

Inez stood on a small rock wall and mounted Terra, whose volatile blue gaze remained fixed on Casper.

"He's going to be trouble," Terra said as he walked to the Running Way.

"He always was."

Inez fitted one of her hands in the grips and stroked the sleek black hair on his muscled shoulders, marveling at the differences between his full-coat and his human skin. To her surprise, she found one as sexy as the other.

He grinned at her over his shoulder. "If you're not too tired when we get back, I am so looking forward to my rubdown."

"I won't be too tired. After all, you're the one doing most of the work. To pass the time in flight, I'll tell you about the kind of rubdown I'll give you."

"Gods, woman, do that and you'll distract me so much we're liable to crash into the sea."

"Should we take the risk?" she teased.

"I'm waiting to hang on your every word."

Inez smiled and fixed her helmet and scarf around her face as they approached the Running Way. As Terra jogged then broke into a full gallop along the packed dirt path, she braced tightly with her knees and held the grips with both hands. Almost before she realized, they were soaring.

* * * * *

Terra beat his wings twice then allowed the wind to carry him for as long as possible. Gatherings weren't like pleasure runs, but were tests of survival. A Horseman would be insane to exert any more energy than necessary when facing such a long journey into weather that could change in a heartbeat. It was bad enough when circumstances forced one to use leg and wing power for most of a journey. Then there was the harvest, which invariably included battles with Ice Lizards, Ridge Snakes, or whatever monstrosity was native to the particular island they landed on.

Though an experienced Carrier, Terra admitted to himself the sensation of Inez astride him was akin to nothing he'd ever felt before. He'd worked with riders he'd liked, but never one he loved. He wanted to protect her, keep her warm, safe and comfortable. He imagined making love with her afterward, of kissing that adorable mouth she had so wrongly called unattractive. When he looked at Inez, he saw nothing but beauty, both of flesh and soul.

He heard wings beating to his left and glanced at the other Horsemen and riders flying around him, all from the Gathering Party. Once the young chestnut Horseman to his left flew ahead, he and Inez were a modest enough distance away for her to release one of the grips and stroke his back and chest. Such contact made his belly tighten with pleasure.

"It's getting colder," she called.

"I can't feel it yet."

He would when they stopped. Other than the fighting, the landing was what he liked least about Gatherings. The Spikeland chill on his sweat-drenched coat was always an irritating shock to his system. While flying, a Horseman didn't notice the cold much, but once the wings stopped beating and the legs stopped grinding, it took a while to stop shaking like a damn flagpole in a windstorm. The Spikelands weren't suited for human or Horseman, just for the few vile beasts dwelling there.

Throughout the ride, he and Inez talked about future plans. She told him of the bathhouse she planned to build. He liked the idea so much he told her not to wait for her own savings. He had more than enough coin to start building right away. He also promised that as soon as they returned, they'd go to the market in the next village where he'd buy her whatever piece of jewelry she'd like for a wedding present.

"What would *you* like for a wedding present?" she called above the wind.

"I already have it!"

"That's sweet, but I want to give you something!"

"Surprise me!"

"All right! I will!"

He grinned, wondering what she'd come up with. Inez was the sort of woman who was always full of surprises.

As the journey went on and the wind grew colder and harsher, more leg and wing work went into play. Terra talked less and concentrated more on breathing. Inez continued talking, and he enjoyed listening. It kept his mind off the grind and boredom of flying, and he loved the sound of her voice. At that moment, he decided no matter where he went or what he did, he'd always want her on his back. Of course there would be times when he'd have to carry others, but he'd always long for her.

The largest island in the Spikelands shone in the distance, but Terra and his party soared over it. Other parties already littered the surface, gathering Rock Blood and fighting Ice Lizards. The white ground was tinged red in places, the blood of beasts and possibly humans and Horsemen as well.

Their destination was a smaller island further north. Several moments later, they hovered over it. They found an area that seemed free of Ice Lizards and landed on a frosty plateau. Old campsites were covered with ice, not that any party remained overnight. Terra and Inez landed first, and he trotted the perimeter of the plateau to ensure it was clear for the others to land. Inez signaled to them that it was safe for the moment then dismounted.

The chill had already set deep in Terra's bones. His throat and chest ached as he panted from his long flight. Sweat seemed to freeze on his gleaming black coat, so he reached for his cloak and extra blanket in his saddle packs.

Inez had already removed them, handing him the cloak and draping the blanket over his back.

"Thanks." He winked at her as he drew the sword from the sheath about his waist. "Gather fast. We might make it out of here without a fight."

Inez smiled at him before joining the other Gatherers and two Horsemen who used picks to dig beneath the ice and snow for the Rock Blood.

Terra and five other Horsemen formed a circle facing outward around the diggers. They remained sharp and on guard, walking constantly to help their overheated bodies cool down from flight yet keep from freezing in the frigid weather.

The first Ice Lizard attacked from the south. Its enormous gray head poked above the plateau. It bared its fangs and uttered a screech loud enough to burst eardrums. Swinging onto the plateau, it attacked, towering above the Horsemen. Terra and another Horseman met its challenge, blocking its clawed strikes with their swords, kicking at it with their rear hooves and driving it back to the edge. A second and third Ice Lizard climbed onto the plateau, not surprising considering they usually traveled in packs.

The lizards seemed particularly desperate for blood, probably because they sensed the Spikes would soon cover the islands, killing the few smaller, thinner-skinned creatures dwelling there. This would mean the lizards would need to live off food stored in their enormous bodies until winter passed and new crops of smaller creatures hatched during the thaw.

"How much longer back there?" Terra bellowed as he and the Horsemen fended off a second wave of lizards.

He'd hoped for a brief period of rest before the journey home, but they wouldn't get it on the plateau. They might be able to find another secluded stretch and wait a few moments, taking off when the lizards discovered them again.

"We're almost done!" Inez called. "Can you hold them off long enough to load up?"

"It's what we do best!" Terra shouted, turning and kicking his back hooves into the lizard he'd been fighting. The creature shrieked as it tumbled off the side of the plateau.

Moments later, they'd cleared the area of lizards. Quickly, the stones were loaded into the Horsemen's saddle packs along with their extra blankets and cloaks so they would be free to fly without hindrance. The party agreed to wait for a short time so the Horsemen could rest before the journey home. When the next lizard poked its ugly face over the edge, the Horsemen agreed flight would be easier than fight.

Inez accepted Terra's arm up. They trotted along the perimeter of the plateau, finding a spot where no lizards climbed, and motioned for the Horsemen to take flight. All except Terra broke into gallops and dove off the clear side of the plateau.

"Ready, love?" Terra glanced at her, warmed by the affection in her dark eyes.

"As I'll ever be."

Glancing up, Terra waited for a signal from one of the Horsemen in flight. The chestnut youth motioned for him to leap from the west edge. Terra galloped and soared straight, so as not to jar Inez as he took off, his wings beating the frigid air.

* * * * *

Inez lay with her cheek against Terra's chest, watching flames leap in the hearth across the room of their cottage.

They'd returned from their journey at noon. After unloading his saddle packs, they'd helped the others carry the cargo into a storage house where Susana, who was the village's primary healer, could inspect it for quality. Inez had walked with Terra while he cooled down and they'd discussed expanding the cottage for when they had children.

"You mean *if* we have children," Inez had said, her hand in his.

"We will."

"You always sound so confident about everything."

"If you want something, you have to believe in it." He glanced at her. "You do want children, don't you?"

"Not before I met you."

The expression in his eyes warmed Inez to her belly. After giving him the rubdown and brushing she'd promised, she'd waited outside the tack house while he shifted shape. He joined her in his Huform and, after sharing a meal at the Chieftain's table, they'd walked home, reaching the cottage at dusk.

Both had decided on an early night, which hadn't happened once they'd started making love. After molding her body into every position imaginable and giving her more orgasms than she managed to count, Terra had finally drifted to sleep.

Inez lay, pleasantly exhausted, but not wanting to sleep yet. She enjoyed the feeling of his warm body against hers and the sensation of his chest rising and falling beneath her cheek.

Never in her life had Inez imagined being so happy.

Drawing lazy shapes across his chest and abdomen, Inez tilted her face to his and found beautiful blue eyes gazing at her.

"I drifted off," he said. "Sorry."

"It's all right. You must have been a little tired."

"The journey was nothing. I've been so obsessed with you I haven't been able to sleep well."

She smiled, her insides warming. "Really?"

"I love you, Inez."

Hearing those words felt wonderful, and she knew he wanted to hear them back. Why couldn't she bring herself to say them? They were three little words, and they were true. She did love him. What was stopping her from confessing aloud when she knew he must sense how she felt?

Rolling her onto her back, Terra buried his lips in her neck. He kissed her from throat to belly, dipping the tip of his tongue into her navel before edging lower. He spread her legs and knelt between them, lifting her buttocks in his hands and covering her clit with his mouth. While he kneaded her backside, he lapped her clit and caressed lower, slipping his tongue into her pussy and licking with deep, upward strokes.

Inez moaned and tangled her fingers in his thick, black curls.

"Terra, oh, don't stop!" she murmured, her eyes squeezed shut as passion grew.

His tongue caressed the moist folds of her flesh, pressed against her throbbing clit and rimmed her pussy lips. Using the tip of his tongue, he teased her perineum and pressed a fingertip to her taut sphincter.

She was on the verge of orgasm when he drew back. She reached for him, but he slipped from her eager hands. Smiling at her over his shoulder, he walked to the table, offering her a perfect view of his smooth, tight buttocks and steely legs. Her brow furrowed, she raised herself on her elbows and watched as he selected a large red apple from the bowl of fruit on the table. Picking up a knife, he began cutting the fruit into paper-thin slices.

"I know Horsemen love apples, but couldn't you wait until after we…you know?"

"I think you'll enjoy this game, Inez. Trust me."

He approached the bed, the apple pieces in his hand and a lustful smile on his lips.

"Lie flat," he said.

Inez did as he asked, drawing a sharp breath as he began placing the cool slices over her warm flesh. He placed the apple over her nipples and between her breasts. He trailed his fingertip over each of her ribs and circled her navel before covering her belly with apple slices.

"Terra!" she giggled, trying not to jerk as he placed the remaining slices along the indentation where her thighs met her groin.

Inez's eyes fluttered closed as his soft lips traveled down her thighs. His tongue traced the shape of each of her kneecaps before he kissed down one calf to her ankle. Taking her foot in his hands, he pressed his strong thumbs to the arch, massaging gently while he kissed the top. He moved to the other foot, kissing, licking and rubbing until she sighed with pleasure.

Had it not been for the fruit covering her body, she might have felt relaxed enough to drift off, but she knew what had to be coming. Her heart thrummed with anticipation that was soon satisfied. Terra loomed over her, one hand braced on either side of her hips. His lips and tongue brushed the sensitive flesh between her thighs and hips as he ate the apples slices resting there. He took his time picking up each slice, chewing slowly and swallowing before taking the next.

"You're right," Inez purred, entangling her fingers in his hair. "I do like this game."

"I've never tasted a more delicious apple," Terra said. "Must be such a shapely plate added sweetness to it."

She gasped, uttering a giddy laugh when he playfully nipped her side before eating the apples slices off her belly. The flat of his tongue ran long and slow between her breasts as he lifted off the slices of fruit.

Inez opened her eyes partway. Only two piece of apple remained, and they covered her nipples. Her heart thrummed wildly. Terra lifted his head, his lips curved upward, his eyes glistening with humor and desire.

"Now I know why Horsemen love apples," she breathed.

A lustful sound rumbled deep in his chest as he bent, his mouth covering one of her nipples and as much of the surrounding breast as he could take in. His tongue swept her nipple, licking away the apple. Raising his head a bit, he quickly chewed and swallowed before doing the same to the other nipple. With the fruit slices devoured, he turned his full attention to her flesh. Taking a nipple between his teeth, he lapped and sucked the stiff little nubbin. Inez writhed, her pussy so hot and wet she thought she might come just from the feeling of his lips and tongue on her breast. She moaned helplessly when he focused on the other nipple. Her heart throbbed in her ears. Her eyes squeezed shut as her feet moved restlessly against the sheets. She was about to explode. She couldn't take another second of his pleasant torture, but she wanted him inside her when she came.

"Terra, please!" she panted, gripping his rock-hard shoulders, trying to force him into her.

He chuckled softly, a sound so utterly masculine she felt torn between frustration and blind desire.

Parting her thighs even more, he settled between them. Two of his long fingers dipped inside her. Slick with her juices, his fingers stroked the sides of her clit.

"Oh, Terra! I can't… I'm going to… Ahh!" she cried out, clinging to him tightly as his cock stroked into her. All it took was that single, long thrust to fling her into orgasm.

Inez's fingers dug into his back and her heels drove into his legs as wave after wave of climax crashed over her.

His breathing grew ragged in her ear as he plunged frantically into her, extending her orgasm and pushing her toward another. His pace never slowed and her next orgasm sent shivers from the roots of her hair to the tips of her toes. With an animalistic cry, he came, every steely muscle in his body tensing, his essence filling her as he panted her name.

I love you, Terra, she thought. *I love you so, so much.*

* * * * *

The following week, Inez and Terra went on three more Gatherings. They worked so well together that Inez actually looked forward to their trips. She'd always felt Gathering was important work, but she never imagined enjoying it so much, in spite of the danger. If ever a Horseman was born to travel, it was Terra. The more his body was challenged, the better he seemed to like it. She still found him arrogant and confident, but he had reason to be. After all, Horsemen were a conceited lot, and many of them didn't have nearly as much to flaunt as Terra did. Aside from his conceit, he was a good man. He was the first to lend aid to human or Horseman if they needed help, and he took careful watch over the Gatherings he led, placing the safety of Inez and his subordinates far above his own. Terra was tough and strict in his leadership, but he was fair. Most of the other Horsemen and Gatherers seemed to like him, even if they did complain about his demanding, no-nonsense manner of running a Gathering. After a bit of wariness on both parts, he and Moor took a particular liking to one another. Being the biggest and most experienced of the village Carriers, they both took their responsibilities seriously, and they both cared about Inez. She was glad the Horseman she looked on as a father and the Horseman she'd taken as a husband got along so well.

Toward the end of the week, the Chieftain received an urgent message that the Plague had broken out in several villages to the east. It was under control and there had been no deaths, but the Rock Blood supply had dwindled badly. Other villages had sent replenishment, but they were also in danger of depletion.

The villages with Gathering Parties were determined to harvest as much Rock Blood as possible before the

Spikes washed the northern islands. To Hornview, that meant more journeys for more Horsemen and Gatherers. A few, like Terra and Moor, traveled daily, while others took up to four journeys a week.

Most of the closest Spikeland islands had been completely harvested and no new Rock Blood would appear until next year. The stronger Carriers were forced to travel further north on longer, rougher journeys, leaving the closer islands for those less experienced.

One day, late in the afternoon, Inez and Terra had just returned from their second journey of the day. A few of the Horsemen had been injured earlier in the week, so Terra and Moor had volunteered to take their place in several Gatherings.

Inez slipped off Terra's back and stretched her stiff legs. Terra shrugged his shoulders, relaxing his tense muscles.

"Lower your head," Inez ordered. He obeyed and she tugged off the loosened Darrion leaf from his nose. She ran her fingertips over his damp chest. His hand, covered in sleek black hair like the rest of his full-coated man body, closed gently over hers.

The weather had gotten worse and the last trip in particular had been difficult, but they were home now. Soon they'd be sprawled comfortably in their bed with firelight dancing on their naked flesh.

"At least we only have one trip tomorrow," Inez said as she began helping Terra unload his saddle packs and fill a sack with Rock Blood.

"Then after that we actually have a day off." He winked. "I wonder how we can spend it?"

"I have a few ideas."

"I bet you do." He grinned, wiggling his ears as he picked up the sack and headed for the storage house.

Inez removed her gloves and helmet as another Gatherer, Dav, approached, looking worried.

"Inez, my Carrier sprained his leg while landing. We had an accident on our Gathering and lost supplies, so we came back to pick up more and this happened. The rest of the party is waiting for us to come back. It's not very far, one of the closer islands. Can I ride your Carrier?"

Inez's brow furrowed. "I don't know, Dav. You'll have to ask him. We just came from two rough journeys today."

Dav narrowed his eyes. "Damn. He might not be up to it. I'd ask Moor, but he went on a late Gathering and won't be back until past midnight."

Terra emerged from the storage house, looking hot. Inez knew he must have been tired, though, she noted with pride, he didn't appear any worse for wear, considering he'd made two journeys that would have knocked a lesser Horseman on his rear.

"Terra," Dav approached, "you wouldn't be up to one more trip, would you? A short one to a close island?"

Inez approached Terra as Dav explained his situation. Terra glanced at her. "Would you mind if I'm late tonight?"

"No, as long as you feel you're up to it."

"Not a problem," he stated, heading for the tack house. "I just want to change the blanket and harness. These are soaked."

"Thanks so much, Terra! I owe you for this," Dav said.

"Yes, and I'll collect." Terra flung him a teasing grin as he walked to the tack house.

Inez followed, unbuckling the girth so he could lift off the saddle. She removed the wet blanket from his back while he unfastened his harness.

"I'll tell Dav I'll ride you back to his party," she said, taking a vial of ointment from Terra's trunk and warming it in her palms before rubbing it into his shoulders and legs.

"No. That's crazy. He knows exactly where his party is, and you must be tired."

"What about you? Three trips in one day? Isn't that pushing it, even for you, Terra?"

"I've done worse, and this is a short trip." He stroked her hair. "I wouldn't go if I didn't think I could fly it safely."

Inez couldn't argue there. She'd seen him perform some risky stunts with no one on his back, but when a Gatherer was involved, Terra played by all the rules.

"Keep the bed warm." He drew her close for a tight embrace before dropping the saddle over a fresh blanket on his back. She tightened the girth and walked outside with him.

Dav waited, mounting from a fence, as he was no taller than Inez. Both men waved to her as they headed for the Running Way. Inez jogged after them, watching the takeoff and wishing Terra was with her instead. She was so selfish when it came to him.

Sighing, she made her way to the bathhouse. She'd go home, tidy the cottage, cook supper and return to the village later. She wanted to be there when he landed, and besides, living in an empty house had lost its appeal to her.

* * * * *

"That was a great crop you brought in from the last Gathering," Susana said to Inez. It was late and the two women spoke softy from where they sat alone at the Chieftain's table. Most of the other villagers and servants had retired for the night, but Inez sat with Susana as she mixed herbal remedies to the flickering of firelight across the room.

"It wasn't easy getting it, believe me."

"I give you Gatherers and Carriers credit, Inez. You're a rugged lot. And speaking of rugged, how's married life?"

"Wonderful."

"Don't look so crestfallen when you admit it."

"But I always said — "

"You'd never marry. I know. I know. Bull dung, is what I say. You love the man. He loves you. That's what matters. He certainly hasn't tried tying you to the house yet."

"He's a wonderful man."

Susana smiled. "That's more like it."

"Susana, I'm so afraid of — " Inez stopped, the words sticking in her throat.

Susana fixed her gaze on Inez, her teasing expression fading. "Of what, Inez? I've never heard you use the word 'afraid' in your life."

"It's silly."

"Tell me."

"I'm afraid of losing him."

"Inez," Susana reached across the table and squeezed her friend's hand, "he loves you. You won't lose him."

"I mean he runs risk in what he does."

"You all do."

"I mean—" Inez sighed, exasperated and confused. She'd never felt so many strange emotions since her path had crossed Terra's. "I mean I love him so much it's almost painful."

Susana's lips flickered upward in a smile. "It's all right, Inez. I've always believed that's how a woman and man should love each other, except don't let it be painful. It's a marvelous thing you share with Terra. And you're lucky. He's a good man."

"Yes, he is."

"Inez, I know you lost your family before their time," Susana said. "I know how it hurts to lose someone you care about, too. Everyone's life ends sometime, even shape-shifters. Enjoy what you have with Terra. Love him and feel his love in return. Have his children, if you can. It'll be a full life even if, heaven forbid, it's for a short time. Trust me. It will be worth it."

Inez forced a smile. Susana was right of course. Even if she lost Terra tomorrow, she wouldn't have traded a moment spent with him.

"Now," Susana donned a happy expression and lifted a mug by her elbow, "to a long, long, happy life to you both—and to me. I hope I find a handsome Horseman—or even a human—to share my life, as well."

"Hear, hear!" Inez lifted her mug and struck it against her friend's. They both took swallows then Inez stood.

"I'm going to check the Running Way. See if they've gotten back."

"Good night, Inez."

"Good night, Susana, and thanks." Inez paused before leaving and glanced over her shoulder. "I hope you find your mate, too."

Susana nodded, a faint smile on her lips.

Outside, Inez glanced with disappointment at the empty Running Way. Except for the torches burning by the Running Way and the tack house, the village was dark. Everyone must have gone to bed.

Suddenly Inez heard wings beating overhead. She craned her neck skyward and her belly fluttered with excitement. Terra and Dav were back.

Terra floated to a perfect landing and trotted to the fence where Inez waited. He panted and lather rolled off his coat. The whites of his eyes shone red from the wind. Dav also looked hot and wind-burned.

"Bad flight?" Inez began helping them unload his saddle packs, noting his heaving flanks. It seemed it would be a while before he was ready to shift back to Huform. "It must have been."

Other Horsemen and Gatherers began landing, all looking worn.

"Short but rough," Dav replied.

"It got stormy," Terra said between pants. "We were flying against the wind."

Once Terra was relieved of his cargo, Dav thanked him again and took the sack to the storage house.

"You better cool off," Inez said reaching up and touching his cheek. Even through the layer of hair, she saw a pulse racing in the pit of his throat. "So much for a short trip."

"If it would have been fine, except for the weather." He turned toward the tack house. "I have to get rid of this damn saddle before I do anything else. I didn't expect to see you in the village."

"I waited for you."

He smiled and reached for her hand. "I'm glad. Once I'm back in Huform, I'll kiss you. Somehow I don't think a face this hairy would appeal to—"

She stood on tiptoe, slipped a hand under the harness on his chest, and tugged his mouth to hers. "Your lips aren't hairy, and I think you're gorgeous in every form."

From the expression in his eyes her reply seemed to please him. They entered the tack house, and he removed his harness, hanging it to dry beside his other one, while she loosened the girth on his saddle. He lifted it off along with the blanket.

"Start your walk," she said. "I'll take care of the tack."

"Thank you." He dropped a kiss on top of her head. He leaned so close she felt heat radiating from his body as he whispered in her ear, "You're a far better rider than Dav. The trip would have been much easier with you on my back."

Inez smiled, watching him until his glistening black body disappeared outside.

When she'd finished with his tack, she found Terra walking around the edge of the Running Way. She joined him, placing a hand on his back and noting he'd already begun to cool. His steps slowed and he took her hand.

"I missed you tonight," she said.

"I missed you, too."

"After our flight tomorrow, I have plans for our day off."

"What plans?"

"Spending the day in bed."

He smiled. "I really like that plan."

"Terra?" Her heartbeat quickened and her entire body tensed at what she was about to say. But hadn't she actually said it before? When Casper had asked why she'd married Terra instead of him, she'd said it was because she wasn't in love with him. Didn't that mean she *did* love Terra?

"Yes?"

"I—"

His gaze fixed on hers and he squeezed her hand.

"I'll rub you down when you're ready."

"Thanks again. You know I live for your rubdowns."

And I live to give them, she thought, *especially on your man half.*

Back in the tack house, Inez layered more of the herbal ointment on her hands and massaged him from neck to hoof. She began at his flanks and worked to his equine shoulders. She paid careful attention to each leg, knowing the muscles must be tired after fighting the wind. She even rubbed his wings, noting the black and white feathers felt even softer than his hair. He'd yet to shift from his full-coat, but she'd grown accustomed to massaging his hair-covered man half. It wasn't as if the hair was shaggy or repulsive, more like a muscular, granite statue covered with a sleek horse's coat. Still, she preferred human skin on his man half—not that she was complaining. Her hands splayed over his broad chest and rubbed his sides. She massaged his shoulders and arms, even his fingers.

Terra watched her as she worked, though his eyes began slipping shut both from the soothing motions of her hands and the fatigue of three hard journeys. *So*, she smiled, tenderly massaging his palms with her thumbs, *he's not invulnerable after all.*

When she turned her back to replace the ointment, she felt the floor shake. She spun, facing Terra who stood before her in his Huform. He removed trousers from his trunk and tugged them on.

"When are you going to let me watch you shift?" she asked.

"Definitely not tonight." He grinned. "I'm too tired."

"It took you about two seconds."

"But it's an enormous expense of energy. Trust me."

"I do. Let's go home."

"That sounds so good." He wrapped his arms around her, his voice rumbling in her ear. "Right now I want a comfortable bed and you in my arms."

"Terra?"

"Yes?" He gazed down at her, stroking wisps of hair from her face.

"I love you," she said quickly, before changing her mind about speaking it aloud.

His lips curved upward and he drew a deep breath. "I love you, too, woman. And—"

"What?"

"I've wanted to hear you say it."

Inez smiled, her body pressed close to his as they left the tack room and headed for home.

Chapter Five
Newcomers

Inez and Terra slept well past dawn on their day off, having returned very late from their journey the previous night. Terra awoke first and stretched, a smile on his face as he glanced at Inez curled up beside him, asleep.

Careful not to wake her, he left the house and bathed in the river. He picked some fresh-scented herbs growing wild among the grass and chewed them after cleaning his teeth. Then he carried buckets of water to the house to heat for her bath. Though winter had yet to touch their village, mornings were still cool, and he knew how much women enjoyed warm baths. He also liked the idea of watching her in it, and perhaps helping to wash her beautiful mass of ebony hair.

He'd just finished filling her wooden tub with warm water when she stirred and sat up in bed, the sheet falling to her waist and baring her rounded breasts. She yawned and stretched. When she spoke her voice sounded husky from sleep. "Good morning."

"I think it will be." He grinned, extending his hand to the tub. "A bath for you."

Inez smiled and stood. "Ohh, I love warm baths. Unless it's frigid cold outside, I'm always too lazy to heat one so I jump in the lake instead. Thank you so much."

"My pleasure." He stared at her shapely backside as she splashed her face and cleansed her mouth with water from a bowl on the table. She nibbled spearmint leaves, and he caught the delicious scent as she approached the tub, stood on tiptoe, and kissed him before sinking into the water.

"Oh, this feels sooo good!" she sighed, closing her eyes and leaning her head back against the tub. He approached with a cake of soap in his hand and dipped it into the water. As he soaped her shoulders and back, she glanced around at him. "I thought we could spend some time at the beach today."

"Great. I like running along the shoreline. The water feels good on the legs." He knelt beside her, lathered his hands with soap, and washed her hair. He used two extra buckets of water to rinse it.

Terra soaped his hands and washed her breasts, paying careful attention to her nipples. They hardened beneath his touch, and his cock jumped in response. Hell, he wanted her!

She placed her wet hands over his, moving them in gentle circles over her breasts. Terra kissed her, his tongue parting her lips.

"I wanted to enjoy this bath," she murmured against his lips, "but now all I want is to be out and wrapped in your arms."

He grinned, dipping his hand between her legs and searching until he found the soap at the bottom of the tub. He washed one of her legs from thigh to foot then massaged his sudsy hands over the other. While he kneaded her heels and caressed her toes, she scrubbed under her arms as well as her more private places. Her clit and pussy ached for him, making them difficult to wash. When she was finally through, he lifted her in his arms, holding her wet body to his dry, naked one and carried her back to the bed.

"The mattress will be soaked!" she protested.

Rather than place her on the bed, he set her beside it and reached for a towel. Terra dried her from head to foot, massaging her back, arms and legs briskly, but tenderly patting her breasts and between her legs. Tossing the towel aside, he knelt in front of her and pressed kisses to her belly as he squeezed her fleshy but firm buttocks. The globes of muscle beneath soft skin felt so good in his hands. He continued rubbing them as he covered her clit with his mouth and licked.

"Terra!" she moaned, winding her fingers through his hair.

His eyes slipped shut as he tickled and caressed. He switched from her clit to her pussy, all the while gripping her pliant bottom cheeks.

Slowly he stood, his body brushing hers. She stared at him, her breathing quick with excitement. With each breath, her nipples brushed his mid-section, the sensation incredibly arousing.

His cock felt hard and ready, but he wasn't in the mood to rush. Making love with a woman took time. A majority of his own pleasure derived from pleasing her. Never in his life had he wanted to excite a woman as he did Inez. She was the most honest and unpretentious female he'd ever known. She was strong and decent. She was his soul mate. He would die for her, if necessary, and he had no doubt she would do the same for him.

He pushed her gently onto the bed, slipped his hands under her arms and positioned her in the center of the mattress. Stretching out on his side across the bed, he guided her legs around his neck, taking a moment to stroke her smooth thighs. He licked her exposed pussy, slipping his tongue between the damp lips and tasting her core. Teasing her clit, he used the flat of his tongue to apply gentle pressure in a steady rhythm.

When she came, her legs tensed, her heels pressing into his shoulders. Her pelvis lifted, and he clutched her hips as he continued lapping and sucking until the final shudder coursed through her. Terra's pulse leapt. The sensation of her tense muscles and the sound of her purrs of desire made his cock feel like an iron bar.

"Umm," she purred, her legs falling from his shoulders as she went limp, her eyes closed. "That was wonderful."

Terra pushed himself onto his knees and grasped her hips. He studied her carefully, enjoying the sight of her full, parted lips and pink-tipped breasts flushed with desire. She gazed at him through coquettish eyes as he pushed his steely cock into her pussy. His eyes closed halfway as he thrust.

"I'd love to hear you right now," he said.

"Hear me?" she sighed as pleasure stirred her body again.

The sight of her hands stroking her breasts made his cock even harder. She pinched her nipples and rubbed them with her thumbs.

"I love hearing you," he breathed when her hands moved from her breasts to his chest. She gently raked her nails over his nipples and he groaned.

"What do you want me to say?"

"Tell me you love me."

Inez's eyes opened wider, staring into his. At that moment she looked so feminine and vulnerable with her lips parted and her rounded body fully exposed to him. Her breasts rose and fell as her passion grew. Still her dark eyes held his with such intensity his heart ached with love nearly as much as his cock ached with desire.

"I love you," she breathed.

"Tell me again," he panted, thrusting harder.

"Oh Terra!" she gasped, her fingers clutching his tense forearms that held her fast as he pounded into her. Her head arched back, her beautiful throat pulsing as she came. "I love you, Terra! I love you!"

He released the reins on his passion into frenzied thrusts, bursting inside her, his hands clutching her satiny hips.

"Gods, I love you woman," he murmured, slipping his spent cock from her body and lying beside her, holding her close.

* * * * *

Hornview was a coastal village, less than two miles from the shoreline. Inez told Terra how much she enjoyed walking on the wet sand and feeling the tide on her bare feet and calves. She sometimes waded in up to her waist, but would go no further. Only a few miles from shore, the man-eating plants spread their prickly leaves, waiting for their next meal.

Terra, in his Huform, walked side by side with Inez over the sand, their feet bare. He'd offered to carry her to the beach, but she wanted to walk with him. He didn't mind. At times he enjoyed his man form as much as his half-equine one, especially during moments like this with his wife. As much as he loved having her on his back—particularly when she was naked with her wet pussy warm against his satiny coat—nothing compared to the closeness they shared while he was in Huform. Only then could he bury his flesh deep inside her and entangle his legs with hers. Nothing felt as good as climaxing inside her, of feeling her pussy palpitate and clench his cock, draining it of his essence.

Simply thinking about making love with her hardened his cock. He paused in walking and tugged off his annoying trousers.

Inez stopped, glancing over her shoulder and lifting an eyebrow.

"You did say it's secluded around here?" he asked

"Yes, but since when is a Horseman shy about nudity?"

"It's not the nudity, but the lovemaking. I don't like an audience when I'm pleasuring my wife."

"Oh." Inez's eyes gleamed with amusement and desire. She tugged off her vest and trousers and approached, splaying her hands across his chest. "I like the sound of that."

He wrapped his arms around her, his cock trapped against her belly as he kissed her. "After we finish with sex, I'm taking you to the market at Gull Cape and buying you the wedding present I promised."

"Umm," she moaned as he kissed her.

Terra closed his eyes and buried one hand in the hair at her nape as he tasted every inch of her mouth. She was delicious and he couldn't get enough of her.

One of her small hands reached between them and grasped his cock. Though her palm was callused from years of holding harness grips, her touch was incredibly delicate. Her fingers fluttered over his cock and he sighed with pleasure.

He stepped away, lying on his back in the sand and spreading his legs as he beckoned her. "Come."

She crawled between his legs, about to take his cock between her lips. It wasn't what he had in mind, but he was unable to resist a few moments of oral stimulation. She licked his cock from base to head and teased the tiny eye with the tip of her tongue. Terra's heart pounded with excitement as she took the tip of his cock between her lips and sucked. As her tongue circled the head, he watched her, forcing his breathing to remain under control as she sucked and licked.

"That's enough!" he commanded before he shot his essence into her skilled mouth. He clutched the root of his cock, drawing several deep, steadying breaths. The fevered moment passed, leaving him aching with desire but back in control. "Sit on me, Inez, your back to me."

He raised his knees, parting them, and she did as he asked, sitting between his legs and using one hand to guide his cock deep into her pussy. She rocked while he caressed her buttocks. The sight of her gorgeous, smooth-skinned bottom jouncing against his belly and the sensation of her hot pussy engulfing his cock were enough to nearly send him into a frenzy. She must have felt the same, for she moaned and shook as she controlled their movements. His hips bucked as he felt his orgasm building deep inside him, firing up his shaft, and erupting into her throbbing pussy.

The tide had reached them, spraying their heated bodies as they ground together, prolonging their ecstasy for as long as possible.

"Since the Plague outbreak, General Sota thought se villages on the northern coast that host Gathering ties might need some reinforcements. Kraig and I were patched here."

"Glad to hear it," Terra said. "We've been overloaded I can use the help."

"I heard you and some of the other Carriers have ltiple flights in a day. Things must be busy."

"I'm sure it's nothing you can't handle, isn't that right, ?" Kraig said. Terra couldn't decide if it was a note of casm or jealousy he heard in his voice. He guessed it s probably a combination of both.

"Whether I can handle it or not, I'd be a fool to refuse p."

Kraig didn't reply as he continued his walk. Casper, o had been listening to the exchange, turned on his heel l left the Running Way.

"Hello," Inez said to Linn.

Terra glanced at her, shaking his head. "Sorry, love. at was rude of me. Inez, this is Linn. Linn, this is my e, Inez."

"Yes." Linn positioned his half-equine body alongside ra and offered Inez his hand. "I heard you and Terra red dreams. I'm glad you were finally able to marry. ngratulations."

"Nice to meet one of my husband's star students."

Linn's brown eyes opened wide in surprise. "Star dent?"

"From what Terra tells me."

"I couldn't say it in training, but you are one of the t," Terra admitted.

As they sat up, Terra squinted skyward, catching sight of two Horsemen passing over them toward the village. They dipped lower and Inez tried concealing her breasts and pubic hair with her hands. Terra pulled her close, covering her naked body until the Horsemen passed. To his surprise, he recognized both the buckskin and the chestnut as two of his most recent trainees from the Hall of Fighting Carriers. What were Linn and Kraig doing in this area?

Terra grasped Inez's clothes and passed them to her. As she pulled on her trousers, she turned her back momentarily. Terra drew a deep breath, closed his eyes and focused all his attention on the area of his lower back known as a Horseman's Turning Point. Shape changing took only seconds, but warranted great effort. Though not painful in itself, the change left him feeling drained for a few seconds. The weak moment passed so quickly it might never have been, and he was settled comfortably in his powerful half-equine form.

"Why do you always *do* that!" Inez turned, stamping her foot. "When are you going to let me watch?"

"Someday." He grinned and tugged her close, bending to kiss her. "I know those two Horsemen headed for the village. I'd like to see what they're doing here."

"Who are they?"

"Two of my students."

"More Fighting Carriers?"

"Recently graduated."

"I'm looking forward to meeting them."

"One of them I'm sure you'll like. Linn. He was one of the best I ever trained. The boy has strength, power, and style. I don't think I've ever seen him perform a bad landing."

Inez smiled as he gave her an arm up. Her legs settled around his sides, her knees gripping him. The sensation was so pleasant he almost told her to remove her trousers and spend the next few hours riding bareback.

"You seem to like him very much."

"He's a good man."

"And the other?"

"Kraig."

"What's he like?" she asked as they headed toward the village.

"Powerful and fast."

"He bothers you, doesn't he?"

"You can tell?"

"No one else probably would," she rubbed the center of his back, "but I know you well, Terra."

"He passed his test without my recommendation."

"Why?" Inez sounded surprised.

"I don't think he showed enough concern for his riders. You know it's a partnership between Gatherer and Carrier. We watch out for each other. One can't imagine himself being more important than the other. Kraig resisted that fact from the first. Oh, after a while he learned the right answers to the questions asked on the test, but memorizing what superiors want to hear and truly believing it yourself are two very different things."

"Why didn't the other instructors listen to you instead of deciding to pass him?"

"Because he had the answers right." Terra [...]
"They look at facts, but sometimes you need to [...] the surface. Another thing, his landings stunk. [...] time I got through with him he made passable [...] and did it right on the test, but he's sloppy. Wor[...] can get you hurt and your rider killed."

"Maybe he's learned more now that he's be[...] his own as a Fighting Carrier."

"I hope so."

The village was a short ride, and Terra [...] between a walk and a jog, pleasant for sharing [...] with Inez, but not particularly challenging. He[...] demands weren't always necessary. Someti[...] enjoyment was just as fulfilling.

When they arrived at the village square, [...] Kraig were walking on the perimeter of the Run[...] to cool down. Moor and Casper had joined th[...] likely for questioning.

As Terra and Inez approached, both n[...] stared in their direction.

Linn smiled and walked toward them, exte[...] hand to Terra who grasped it in a warm handsha[...]

"It's good to see you again, Sir," the youth [...] dark blond hair had escaped from its braid and [...] damp waves on the breeze. Always a large boy, [...] to have put on even more muscle since Terra ha[...] him, probably due to an increase in flights.

"Good to see you, too, Linn. Kraig." Terra [...] the redhead's direction. The youth's green eyes [...] Terra. The young fool always had a bad atti[...] apparently it hadn't gotten any better. Terra f[...] attention back on Linn. "What are you two doing[...]

Linn smiled, genuine gratitude in his expression. "Thank you, Sir."

"You're no longer a new recruit, Linn. Call me Terra."

"Yes, Sir."

Terra chuckled, and shook his head as he fell into step alongside Linn. Moor joined them, and all four had a long conversation about past flights and Gatherings. Finally, they brought Linn to meet the Chieftain. Kraig was leaving the longhouse as they arrived. He stalked past them without so much as a glance as he headed for the bathhouse.

Inside, Moor introduced Linn to the Chieftain who said he was glad more Horsemen had arrived. Terra knew this was only a partial truth. Yes, they needed help, but the more Fighting Carriers joined their Gatherings, the less profit for the Chieftain.

Inez slipped off Terra's back and joined her yellow-haired friend, Susana, who was mixing herbs over the fire. The young healer couldn't seem to keep her eyes from Linn, and Terra nearly laughed aloud at the blush that crept into Linn's high cheekbones each time he glanced at Susana. Terra watched from across the room, one front foot crossed over the other, as Linn approached the healer after finishing his conversation with the Chieftain.

"Who are you?" the young man asked.

Susana stared up at him and licked her lips as if they'd suddenly gone dry. "Susana."

"I'm Linn."

"And I'm in the way." Inez grinned, leaving the two alone as she joined Terra.

Inez stood close to Terra, placing a hand on his withers as she remarked, "I think love is blooming."

"I guess they like each other," he said, slipping an arm around his wife's shoulders and kissing the top of her head.

"They make a cute couple."

"Speaking of that, I owe you a wedding present." Terra clasped her hand as they walked to the door. Outside, he waited by a fence while Inez mounted. They headed out of Hornview toward a village he knew had one of the best markets around.

* * * * *

"Just what this village needs. More Horsemen." Casper's lip curled as he stepped into the tack house and approached the newly arrived Fighting Carrier, Kraig.

Just standing in the tack house was enough to turn Casper's stomach. He detested the hulking beasts who called themselves Horsemen. Their species disgusted and frustrated him. Why did so many people look on them like gods, particularly stupid women?

"What do you want, *human*?" Kraig sneered. The beast's hostility was almost tangible. Grudgingly, Casper had to admit he liked that.

"You have a problem with humans?"

Kraig looked down his wide nose at Casper. "I have no use for humans. Your women are only necessary as dams for our children. Other than that, you're weak, pathetic, disease-ridden insects."

"Strong words from an ignorant, stinking horse."

Kraig pulled his sword and advanced on Casper who backed away.

"Cut me and you won't hear my proposition!"

"What could you possibly have to offer me?" Kraig stopped, the tip of his sword pressed to Casper's throat.

"I saw how you looked at Terra. You don't like him any more than I do."

"What's it to you?"

"He married the woman who should have been mine," Casper seethed. If he thought he had the power to challenge Terra in an out-and-out fight, he'd have done it long ago. He knew he hadn't, but with the coming of the new Horsemen and Kraig's obvious hatred of Terra, a plan for revenge had formed in his mind.

"Do I look like I care?" Kraig snarled.

"Not about me, but how do you feel about Terra? You really hate him, don't you? And he was your teacher."

"He was a fool who couldn't see that a Carrier's first responsibility is to himself!"

"Is that all?"

"No. The condescending bastard criticized my landings."

Casper laughed. "Your landings? I asked some questions about you, and from what I heard your landings have already killed one Gatherer and wounded two others."

"They were lousy riders!"

"You're on probation with the Fighting Carriers. You run the risk of being banished from their ranks."

"I can out-fly any Horseman I know!"

"Even Terra?"

Kraig's teeth ground visibly and his fists clenched. "Maybe."

Casper shrugged. "You can't outfight him though, or I'm guessing he'd be dead by now."

"I might be able to beat him."

"But you're not sure?"

"The man's as strong as a fucking Ice Lizard!"

"But if he happened to die, you would shed no tears over him?"

Kraig's lips twisted in a humorless smile. "I would celebrate."

"Do you feel any loyalty to him at all?"

"Loyalty? Hah!" Kraig scoffed.

"If I told you there's a chance to get rid of Terra, would you assist?"

"Wait." Kraig narrowed his eyes at Casper. "Did he put you up to this? Is he trying to find another reason to blacken my name before General Sota and the rest of the Fighting Carriers?"

"I would sooner eat shit than work with him in any way," Casper said. "I have a plan that will rid us of Terra."

"And his woman?"

"She'll be dead along with that horse's ass she married."

"I thought you wanted to marry her?"

"Not after she's been with a Horseman."

"I don't know how he could bring himself to fuck her anyway. She has teeth like a true-horse. So tell me how you plan to destroy Terra? I warn you, he's an amazing fighter. I can vouch for his strength and endurance."

"He's powerful," Casper shrugged, "but everyone has their limit. Even the mighty Terra. My plan will take patience. It's not to be rushed. We must wait for the perfect moment for it to work."

"I have patience."

"Good."

"Because I've chosen to go through with this doesn't mean I think any better of you, *human*."

"Nor I of you, *beast*. It's only to get rid of Terra and his slut Inez."

"Agreed. Now get out of here. I need to change shape."

* * * * *

"I love my gift," Inez said, admiring the gold and ruby cuff bracelet on her wrist. "I've never had such a nice piece of jewelry before."

"I couldn't imagine it on a more beautiful wrist." Terra glanced over his shoulder at her. "You have me curious, though. What did you buy at that old woman's cart while I was getting us something to eat?"

Inez grinned and massaged the base of his neck. "I'll show you tonight. It's a surprise."

"I love surprises."

"You'll like this one," she murmured, pressing kisses across his back. Once they'd left the village for the freedom of the meadows, she'd removed her trousers and shirt to ride him bareback. The afternoon had grown rather hot and sunny, and he looked forward to a swim in the lake behind their cottage.

"I don't know about you, but I'm in the mood for a run," he said, "and a nice stretch of the wings before supper."

"Umm, sounds good to me," she purred, her arms slipping beneath his and wrapping around his torso. He felt her knees grip his back tighter, her silken legs pressing against his short coat. Already he felt dampness from her pussy against him and he sighed.

Terra had always loved running, testing himself, but traveling with Inez made running a whole new and even more fascinating experience. Fast runs with her naked on his back aroused him as much as her. He'd race until she came, and that in itself would keep him hard until they made love, either right away or later that night.

"Ready?" he asked.

"Oh yes!" She nibbled his neck and ran her tongue across his back.

Terra cantered and moments later broke into a full gallop. His powerful legs devoured the ground. His wings pressed close to his sides as he ran. He could have galloped for hours before feeling much of a challenge, so he forced himself faster. Chunks of dirt and grass flew beneath his hooves as he reached the top of his speed, holding it for as long as he could. Inez's palms pressed against his chest, her fingers slipping as his skin grew wet. Her warm breasts and belly felt so good on his sweat-slicked back. Her nipples were hard, and he felt her heart beating against his back before his own pounded so loud it filled his ears. Gods, it felt good to run, completely free, with the woman he loved writhing on his back.

Terra leapt, his wings opening wide and beating as he rose high. His legs continued racing on air, propelling them fast across the sky. Wind stung his eyes and it took a moment before the blurriness faded.

"Oh, Terra!" Inez called, her arms and legs clinging to him tightly. "This is so fast!"

"Like it?" he shouted.

"Love it! Can't you feel?"

He could. Her dampness mingled with the sweat on his back. Blood pumped fast through Terra's excited body. Tonight he would be so ready for her!

All too soon, their cottage shone below, a grayish speck in the lush field. Rather than land, he circled the field three more times before slowing his legs and straightening his wings to coast for a moment.

Though his breathing was labored, it wouldn't take long to return to normal. He was in excellent physical condition and flights of many miles at top speed were only part of his continued training.

"I still can't believe how fast you are," Inez sighed, her arms loosening on him. He felt the last remaining throbs ripple through her. As he circled the field two more times, allowing his pulse to slow, she languidly caressed his shoulders, back and chest. Her bare feet stroked his sides and she wiggled her lovely little bottom against his slick coat. He could scarcely wait to be lying in bed with her, buried deep in her hot, wet pussy.

"Hang on," he told her.

"Why?"

"I'm landing in the lake."

Inez's arms tightened around him as he descended. The cool water jarred his heated body at first, but after the initial shock it felt marvelous. He swam with her on his back until she slipped off him and they both waded to shore.

As Inez walked ahead of him, Terra changed form, his eyes momentarily slipping shut. When he opened them, he found Inez standing in front of him, gazing up at him. Taking her face in his hands, he kissed her, stroking her tongue with his. She stood on tiptoe and slipped her arms around his neck. He allowed her to take control of the kiss as she began sucking hard on his tongue. A shiver of desire ran down his spine, settling in his Turning Point. Pressing and caressing the Turning Point was often enough to fling a Horseman headlong into orgasm, while striking it caused shattering pain. As if sensing his need, her hands slipped from his neck, down his ribs, and around his waist. Pressing her palms against his lower back, she massaged his Turning Point in a deep, sensual rhythm that soon had him panting.

"I can't wait until we get home. I want you right here. Right now," he said in a husky voice.

"I won't argue," she breathed, then shouted in surprise when he dropped onto the grass, yanking her with him. She landed on his chest, her nose touching his. Cupping her head in his hand, he gently pressed her closer, kissing her. Her breasts felt so soft, except for her pebble-hard nipples that rubbed against his chest. She tasted warm and delicious. One of her small hands reached between them and stroked the rock-hard length of him before she grasped his balls.

"You know what I want, woman?" he asked between kisses.

"Show me?"

A groan of desire escaped his throat as he sat up, grasping her waist and pushing her to her knees. Inez seemed to immediately understand. Positioning herself on her hands and knees, she offered him a perfect view of her rounded buttocks.

"Mmm," he purred, kneeling behind her and cupping a firm yet fleshy bottom cheek in each hand. He kneaded and caressed, then bent and kissed each soft, warm globe before running his lips over her entire back. As he kissed up her spine and between her shoulder blades, he inched forward, rubbing his cock over her rear. He moaned again as the tip ran along the indentation between her bottom cheeks. He straightened for a moment, bracing his hands on her waist and tugging her closer as his steely rod slid, inch by inch, into her magnificent pussy.

Terra's eyes closed halfway and he fought to control his breathing. Damn, this felt so good! She was tight, hot and oh-so-wet! She moaned, trying to wiggle closer to him, her internal muscles clenching his cock until he thought he might burst right then and there.

While one of his hands remained firm on her waist, he used the other to stroke her ribs and belly, enjoying the smoothness of her skin. He stroked her clit as he thrust into her with frustrating slowness. He wanted to plunge fast and hard, but he needed to reestablish his control. Drawing several steadying breaths, he focused his gaze on her, concentrating solely on pleasuring her.

"Oh, Terra!"

"I'm here."

"Gods, I know!" she giggled, the lust in her voice exciting him to a fevered pitch, still, he only increased his thrusting enough to push her closer to orgasm. Her pussy throbbed around his cock. Her moans turned to sobs of pure ecstasy as his fingers rubbed her clit, drawing out her orgasm. His thrusts never ceased, but continued nudging her toward a second climax.

"Terra! Oh, damn it!" she panted, clutching handfuls of grass as her hips and buttocks jerked, meeting his more powerful thrusts.

"I'm sorry," he stopped, his heart pounding and his cock aching with desire. "I didn't mean to hurt you."

"Believe me, you're not hurting me! Keep going!"

Terra's belly clenched and his chest expanded as he drew a deep, passionate breath. This woman was *made* for him! His perfect dream lover, who enjoyed baring her beautiful buttocks to him and accepting massive thrusts as he claimed her on the sun-warmed grass!

He ran his palms up her sides and cupped her breasts, kneading and stroking, his thumbs and forefingers rolling her spiky nipples. Dipping his head forward, he nipped and licked her shoulders. "I want to eat every inch of you, woman."

"Oh yes, Terra! I want you to eat every inch of me!"

Again he grasped her waist and threw back his head as he slammed into her, the world turning black and his heart pounding in his ears. His teeth clenched, he tried holding his orgasm at bay until she reached hers, but he wasn't sure he could make it. Suddenly her body convulsed and she cried out, her throbbing pussy squeezing his cock, drawing out his essence, leaving him momentarily spent.

As his breathing returned to normal, Terra slipped from her, allowing her to completely collapse on the grass. Rolling her onto her back, Terra knelt between her legs, licking her moist slit that still twitched with the final throes of her climax.

Inez moaned softly, her eyes opening halfway. "Oh, Terra, this feels so good."

He couldn't reply since his mouth was too busy with her clit and pussy. He ran the tip of his tongue down both sides of her clit before thrusting his tongue inside her. The rich scent of her love musk filled his nostrils and the taste of her drove him to madness. Already his soft cock was swelling with need for her body as his heart swelled with love for her entire being.

When he sensed by her quick breathing and squirming hips she was close to orgasm, he sat up and entered her with a long, slow thrust.

Inez stiffened, her pussy tightening around his cock as her head arched back against the ground. As Terra thrust, he used one hand to fondle her breasts and the other to caress her clit. This time her pleasure seemed so intense that Terra thought she must have slept for a few moments after. Her eyes opened and she watched as he rubbed his steely cock over her entire body.

"Oh, I like this," she purred.

"So do I," he breathed, tensing as pleasure grew. He rubbed his cock head over her thighs and across her belly. Moving upward, he knelt above her and swirled the hard, ruddy staff over her breasts. Her nipples scraped the head, the sensation marvelous. She moved beneath him, and suddenly the tip of his cock was swallowed by a warm, wet cavity. Her mouth closed over his cock, her teeth gently worrying the sensitive flesh, her tongue swirling over the head. She sucked deeply, applying steady pressure that soon had his heart racing as if he'd just come from a long, hard journey.

Her hand closed over his balls, squeezing and kneading the heavy sac.

"You're going to kill me, woman!"

"Umm," she purred, still licking and squeezing. Reaching up, she grasped his buttocks, her fingers gripping tightly. Two fingers pressed against his sphincter. She moved her hand upward, pressing his Turning Point. Almost unendurable sensation flooded his body. Terra groaned, his muscles stiffening as he fought the orgasm that threatened to unman him. Somehow he mastered his emotions and slipped down her body. His cock felt close to bursting as he thrust inside her. Inez's knees squeezed his thighs, much like she squeezed his back when they flew together.

"Inez, oh, Inez!" he panted, thrusting faster as her feet pressed him closer.

Her hips matched his rhythm and she moaned, her fingers biting into his shoulders and back. Knowing she was close, he fought off his climax, every muscle tight as his body strove for release. At the first ripple of her orgasm, he drove into her with a vengeance, crying out her name as he came. His entire body went limp atop her until she squirmed.

"You're squashing me!" she giggled.

"I'm sorry." He rolled off her immediately and drew her to his side.

Inez cuddled against him, her eyes slipping shut. He gazed at her, his mind still pleasantly relaxed from his orgasm, and brushed wisps of hair from her forehead. Gods, he loved her so much it was like an ache inside him that could only be satisfied by holding her, talking to her and being with her.

He stood, Inez still in his arms. She clung to his neck and kissed the hollow of his throat. "I love you Terra."

"I love you, too," he said softly, kissing her forehead as he carried her to their cottage.

Chapter Six
The Rescue

Back at the cottage, Terra placed Inez on the bed and stretched out beside her. She smiled at him and stood.

His gaze swept her naked back and buttocks as she walked to the table and picked up her small leather travel bag she'd yet to unpack from their trip to Gull Cape.

She wore a seductive grin that piqued his curiosity. "It's time I showed you what I bought."

Terra raised himself onto his elbow as she emptied the contents of the bag on the bed. There were three wooden containers and several lengths of black and red silk. Though he wasn't precisely sure what she had in mind, he knew he was going to love it. Already his cock stirred and his belly tightened with anticipation.

"Scented oil," she explained, uncorking one of the containers and holding it out to him. He sat on his knees and sniffed the contents.

"Umm," he smiled, "apple."

She offered him another. It smelled of clover, and the third a combination of vanilla and honey.

Leaning forward, she whispered against his lips, "Would you like another rubdown right now, in Huform?"

He nodded, slipping his arms around her and kissing her. Their tongues slashed one another for a moment before she placed her palms to his chest and pushed. She couldn't have moved him, but he relented, watching her curiously. She chose a piece of black silk and slipped behind him. His heartbeat quickened when she placed the silk across his eyes and tied it in back of his head.

"Can you see?" she asked.

"Not a thing."

Her arms slid beneath his and she gripped his chest, her breasts crushed against his back, like when she rode him bareback. Her tongue traced the shape of his ear before she whispered, "Do you trust me?"

"Yes."

"Good. Lie on your stomach."

He did as she asked, his cheek pressing against the pillow, his vision blackened by the silk.

"Place your hands behind your back," she ordered. He obeyed and seconds later felt more silk wrapping around his wrists. She tied him snugly.

His heartbeat quickened. This game was strange, but it appealed to him. He wondered if she knew he could break the silken bonds whenever he felt like it, or did she believe she had him in a helpless position?

Terra didn't realize how helpless he was—at least to his own desire—until her delightful ministrations began. She took one of his feet in her hands and pressed her lips to the sole. She kissed the entire bottom of his foot while her small fingers, slick with clover-scented oil, massaged his ankle and instep. Her kisses moved up his calf to the back of his knee where she licked the sensitive indentations at the joint. She paused for a moment, and the next sensation was of oil dripping on the back of his thigh. Her palms ran over his thigh, kneading the muscles with slow, strong strokes. Terra resisted the urge to moan aloud. His rock-hard cock ached where it lay trapped between his belly and the bed. Inez stopped massaging his thigh and shifted position. He felt her kisses on the sole of his other foot, and this time he did utter a low groan of pleasure. She kissed and rubbed his calf and again used her tongue on the back of his knee. Her warm palms, slick with oil, caressed his thigh.

Nudging his legs apart, she knelt between them and covered his buttocks with kisses.

"Oh Gods, Inez, you're driving me mad!" he growled.

"Umm," she moaned softly. "I never thought I'd actually want to kiss a man's ass."

His chuckle mingled with hers and he tugged at his bonds.

Her hand rested on top of his wrists. "Don't. Let me finish."

"You're going to finish me all right!" He panted with anticipation when he felt her oiled hands rubbing his bottom, squeezing the hard globes of muscle. One of her slick fingers slipped between his bottom cheeks and pressed against his sphincter. He groaned again, his cock swelling and pulsing. A completely helpless sound burst from his lips when her oiled fingers and palms swept his lower back, directly on his Turning Point. The mysterious atmosphere combined with her sensual touches drove him to a level of passion he'd never known. He hoped he wouldn't waste the moment by coming on the mattress instead of buried deep inside her.

Slippery, oil-scented hands pushed aside his thick hair and slid over his ribs and across his back. She straddled his back, her buttocks resting against his as she kneaded the muscles in his shoulders and arms. Her breasts flattened against him while she licked and kissed his nape.

Inez licked both of his ears and massaged his scalp before slipping off him. She untied his hands. Rolling over, he reached for her, but she eluded his grip.

"I'm not finished yet," she said. "There's still your front to do."

He groaned. "I don't know if I can make it, woman."

"You'll make it, you big, powerful Fighting Carrier. I know the kind of control you have."

"Don't taunt me in the state I'm in." He grinned, grasping his pole-hard erection in one hand and pumping it a couple of times.

He allowed her to guide his hands above his head where she again bound his wrists. She kissed his forehead and over each blindfolded eye. Playfully, she took the tip of his nose in her teeth before kissing him full on the mouth. Her tongue stroked his while her hands gripped his chest. Again she straddled him. This time his steely cock wedged between her bottom cheeks as she slowly rubbed her oiled hands over his shoulders, arms and chest. Suddenly she sat up a bit and guided his cock into her sopping pussy.

Terra didn't even try controlling his moans of pleasure when she began riding his cock while her palms stroked his torso. Could she feel his heart knocking against his ribs? She must have, for it beat so fast he felt as if he'd just come from a journey to the Spikelands against the wind. Her fingertips trailed up and down his underarms. She used her fingernails to gently scrape his nipples as her pace increased. She was also moaning, and he had the uncontrollable urge to caress her breasts and grasp her waist.

With a swift tug, the silk broke. He dragged off the blindfold and stared at Inez. Her head was thrown back, her bouncing breasts thrust forward as she rocked and writhed atop him. He took her breasts in his hands, gently pinching and squeezing her nipples, before he grasped her waist as she shouted his name and came, pulsing around his cock.

With several hard, upward thrusts, he came, spurting into her, his breath rasping and pulse thumping wildly.

Inez melted onto his chest, her parted lips resting against his neck, her breath fanning his skin.

"Gods, woman, we should go to the market more often."

Inez giggled and squeezed him, her legs entangled with his.

* * * * *

The following afternoon Inez tidied the house, which had been badly neglected since the extra Gatherings had begun. She and Terra had returned from the Spikelands a few hours ago. They had only one journey planned that day, but again Terra agreed to replace an injured Horseman. He'd joined Moor's party and Inez didn't expect him home until later that night.

As she glanced out the window to watch the progress of the workers installing the bathhouse, she noticed Susana walking toward the cottage, looking worried. Inez's heart dropped to her belly. Something had happened to Terra and the healer was bringing her the bad news!

She raced to the door and flung it open, meeting Susana halfway down the cobbled walk.

"Inez! I was hoping you'd be home. I want to talk to you."

"Is something wrong?" Inez wondered if she sounded as panicked as she felt.

"Yes and no."

"Terra?"

Susana's brow furrowed, then she grinned. "Heavens no. You *do* fawn over the man, don't you?"

"No." Inez clenched her teeth, feeling both stupid and relieved.

"I don't blame you for fawning," Susana continued. "I guess it's what you're supposed to do when you meet the man of your dreams—quite literally in your case."

"How about you? I've noticed you and Linn have gotten quite friendly." Inez tossed her a knowing glance.

Susana's smile faded. "That's what I came to talk about."

"Come in. I'll make us some tea—or by the look of you, maybe you'd prefer a good belt of wine?"

"I'd take the wine if I didn't have more rounds to make in the village."

"So what is it about Linn? You two seem to get along well."

"I do. *We* do."

"What then?"

"You know I've always been attracted to Horsemen. I mean, they're the most sensual creatures in the world."

"You don't have to convince me." Inez grinned.

"I'm not a bigot."

"Whoever said you were?"

"It's just that I've heard some talk in the village and—
"

"What kind of talk?" A strange feeling settled in Inez's stomach.

It wasn't that she cared what other people thought, but bigotry infuriated her, both in humans and Horsemen. Though most people considered the Horsemen a noble race and thought it an honor for a woman to mate with one, some people, like Casper, harbored prejudice against them. She and Terra were the focus of attention, not all of it good, that she knew, but no one except Casper had made comments directly to them. Probably because they feared Terra's strength and Inez's temper. Their positions as a Fighting Carrier and senior Gatherer also commanded respect in the village.

"Some people have said Linn and I are going to be the next to mate and then the village will have two permanent Fighting Carriers."

"That's not so bad." Inez relaxed. *At least it would be less work for Moor and Terra.* "Linn's a great flyer and from what I've heard, a strong fighter."

"Oh, he is." Susana's eyes glowed. "Have you ever watched him land? I bet it's just how a warrior angel would look. He's so graceful for a Horseman of his size."

Inez grinned. "So far I haven't heard any problems."

"I'm a healer."

"I'm aware of that."

"I've cared for Horsemen as well as humans. I know their bodies, I—"

"What?"

"I've never touched one outside of performing my duty. I've done plenty of dreaming about what it might be like being with one. What is it like, Inez?"

"Well," Inez sighed. While she didn't want to disclose intimate details about her sexual relations with her husband, she knew Susana needed an answer, some kind of reassurance or encouragement. "In his Huform, he's exactly like a man. As you said, you're a healer. You know that. I will say Horsemen's tremendous stamina doesn't seem to fade with their beast-form, if you get my meaning."

"Really?" Susana leaned forward a bit.

"Oh yes. He can go morning, noon and night with little rest in between. The only time he gets tired is directly after Gatherings, or if he's had more than one Gathering a day."

"I guess my concern is that I've never ridden a Horseman."

"Oh." Inez forced a smile. She'd been supplying the wrong kind of information. Since marrying Terra, her thoughts dwelled on lovemaking.

"I'm afraid of heights."

Inez raised an eyebrow. "Not a good thing when a Horseman's courting you. Did you tell him? Linn looks like an understanding man."

"I've been too embarrassed, especially after all the comments I've always made about my attraction to Horsemen in general."

"It's nothing to be ashamed of. Once you start flying, I guarantee you'll love it. Linn is the right Horseman to show you. Terra can't brag enough about his performance as a recruit."

"I can't believe this." Susana ran a hand through her hair. "Just a short time ago I was convincing you that being with Terra was the right thing to do. Now here I am, acting like a scared chicken over being with Linn."

"Well, just relax and enjoy what comes."

"It's not just the flying, either. What about the dreams? Linn and I have never shared dreams. What if I fall in love with him and suddenly he finds the woman he's meant to be with?"

"Not all Horsemen share dreams. Many have mated with a human woman whom they've never dreamed of. And the dreams might come for you. Where is it written that dreams occur before the couple meets?"

Susana's brow furrowed. "That's true. Do you and Terra still share dreams?"

"Not since we've mated," Inez admitted. Though at times she missed the dreams, the reality of being with Terra was a fair price to pay for their loss.

"You're still happy, though?"

"I've never been happier."

"Well," Susana stood, sighing, "I have to get back to the village."

"I'll go with you. It's almost dusk and the Gathering Party will probably be returning soon. Do you need any help on your rounds?"

"That would be great."

* * * * *

"That was a rough party!" Dav bellowed to Terra above the roar of wind as they soared across the Spikelands.

"Too many Ice Lizards!" Terra shouted in reply.

"It's too bad Moor got hurt. I hope he makes it."

Terra could empathize with Moor flying home with a Gatherer and cargo even though he'd taken quite a swipe across his arm. The wound was positioned well, because while Horsemen often used their arms for momentum, they weren't as necessary to flying as legs, hindquarters, and wings. It was the blood loss that concerned Terra. Before they'd managed to stanch the flow, Moor had lost quite a bit of blood. They'd allowed him to rest as long as possible while the other Horsemen fought off the lizards. He said he was able to travel—not that he had much choice. That was the danger of flying, especially in the Spikelands. In the tropics, a party might be able to hole up in a cave for the night, but the Spikelands were completely barren, leaving anything that breathed vulnerable to the lizards.

Terra glanced ahead to Kraig and his Carrier. The red-haired Horseman's full-coat gleamed, even in the murky sky. The youth was one of the fastest Carriers Terra had ever known, and the boy flaunted his speed often. That could prove troublesome if he ever tired himself and ended up fighting severe weather with his strength depleted. That had been a lesson Terra had learned all too well his first year out as a Fighting Carrier. He'd broken the record for the fastest flight to the northern-most Spikeland and back—a record that still stood—but had nearly killed himself in the process. By the way Kraig flew, he wouldn't doubt the youth preparing himself to attempt breaking Terra's record in this year's race.

Terra's gaze swept to his right, left, up, and down as he checked the rest of his party. Only Moor was out of his view.

"Can you see Moor behind us?" Terra shouted to Dav. He assumed the injured Carrier was sensibly keeping a slow pace.

He felt Dav shift on his back as he looked behind them. "Yes, he's there. Looks okay—wait! His Gatherer's unloading their cargo!"

Terra muttered a curse, his gut tightening with concern. Moor must have been desperate for his Gatherer to toss the precious Rock Blood to the sea below.

"Terra, he's dropping fast!" Dav bellowed.

Must be the blood loss after all, Terra thought, instructing Dav to brace himself as he turned in midair and sank after Moor who was desperately trying to keep a safe level above the sea. The brown Horseman gasped visibly, his eyes unfocused and his ears pinned close to his head. Blood had seeped through his bandaged arm. Terra guessed if he could fly for himself, he might make it home. His Gatherer flung Terra a desperate look that confirmed his guess. Already the man clung to the harness with one hand while trying his best to unbuckle the saddle with the other.

"I'm going to fly in close beside them!" Terra told Dav. "You help his Gatherer onto my back!"

"What?" Dav shouted, shock in his voice. "Are you sure you can carry the two of us home?"

"It's either that or those two are as good as dead. Moor won't make it!"

One of the other Horsemen, slimmer than Moor and Terra, had dropped to Moor's opposite side. His Gatherer signaled to Terra that they were ready to help.

The rescue proved difficult, since Terra had to move in quite close to Moor without striking either the Horseman or his rider. Dav's strong legs pressed hard to his sides as the man leaned behind Terra's beating wings and reached for the other rider. The struggle for the second man to find his seat on Terra's back threw off his momentum and Terra fought to keep from turning precariously in the strong winds. He was grateful the wind blew at his back. If it had been facing them, he might have had his doubts about making the rest of the long journey home with two Gatherers and cargo on his back.

A glance at Moor revealed the wounded Carrier had already thrown off his saddle. The other Horseman and Gatherer had tossed him a leather strap that he fitted under his front equine-legs. The other Horseman held the strap and flew above Moor. If the injured party felt he needed rest, he could take a moment or two to lean into the strap while the Horseman above helped support him. Moor didn't seem ready to burden the other Horseman, however, and continued flying on his own, apparently more in control now that the saddle and Gatherer were off his back.

"How are you holding up?" Dav called to Terra.

"Fine!"

Dav didn't speak again, knowing Terra needed to reserve his wind for the flight. Kraig appeared a short distance away, glaring at Terra through eyes turned red as his coat due to the wind. His lip curled as he stretched his legs and beat his wings, soaring ahead.

Terra should have used his influence sooner as a top-ranking Fighting Carrier to have Kraig sent to another village, but other than his personal dislike of the man, he had no legitimate complaint—until now. Kraig did his share of work and, other than some deliberately rough landings, did it well. Still, there was more to Gathering than speed and the ability to carry cargo. The entire group depended on each other for survival. One rock in a hoof and the whole horse could fall. It was the same for a Gathering Party. One bad Carrier or Gatherer, and everyone suffered.

The wind shifted, and Terra leveled out, doing his best to conserve his energy. The weight of two men plus cargo wasn't too distracting at first, but they were still far from home. After an hour, the extra burden began telling on him. Instead of the steady breaths he liked to keep for most of his flight, he began panting sooner than usual. His chest ached as his lungs worked in the cold. His pulse was much faster than he would have preferred at that time in the journey.

"Do you want me to get rid of the cargo?" Dav shouted.

"No, I'm fine!" Terra called, if just to prove to himself he still had breath enough to talk. If he couldn't talk, then he might consider dropping cargo.

Kraig's pumping hindquarters were visible above. Being a large Carrier, Terra knew he had the strength to hold a second rider, even for a short time. If their positions had been switched, Terra would have offered to relieve him of his extra weight halfway through the journey. He knew the other Horsemen on the journey didn't have the power to carry two riders, still they'd flown in close a few times and offered him a support strap that he refused.

Terra had flown with heavy cargo before, as did every Fighting Carrier he'd ever trained, Kraig included. He felt it was important for them to prepare for every possible situation. Not only that, if one of the smaller Horsemen tried using a support strap to hold up someone of his size, fully loaded, it was a sure way for both them and their riders to crash.

The wind weakened as they left the far north, and for the first time, Terra wished for those cold winds. At least they'd been at his back and helped in the flight. For the last miles, he'd be using his own power. By the time they hovered over the home shoreline, he never thought a Running Way looked so good. His throat ached from gasping though an open mouth when nose breathing simply couldn't supply him with enough air. His heart throbbed in his ears and he dripped sweat from head to hoof.

"We're almost there," Dav said, more as an offer of support than a necessary comment.

Though tired and concerned about Moor, Terra had to admit feeling a bit of pride as he circled to land. As a Fighting Carrier, he was still top-notch.

* * * * *

Inez and Susana had joined Linn in polishing his saddles and harnesses. Inez worked on Terra's, thinking he'd be happy to already have it done. She ran her hands over a leather harness, remembering how it felt to hold it as she rode him. She liked how it smelled of polish and his own sensual musk.

"Carriers are landing!" Came a shout from outside the tack house. "Looks like one's injured!"

"Gods!" Inez dropped the harness and ran. Linn and Susana, her leather bag of healing supplies in her hand, followed close behind. The young Fighting Carrier broke into a gallop, passing the much slower humans as they raced to the Running Way.

Inez's heart pounded with fear. Terra had been wounded. She knew it!

As they approached the Carriers who'd landed, she saw it wasn't Terra, but Moor on his knees. He gasped so loudly she heard it long before she and Susana reached him. Linn and another Horseman knelt beside him, supporting him before he collapsed completely.

"There's blood all over him. Where's it coming from?" Inez said, feeling Moor's steaming, bloody torso for the wound.

"Arm," Moor forced out between wheezes.

Susana had already found the injury and removed the blood-soaked bandage. She told Inez to pass her another. While Susana worked, Inez rubbed Moor's overheated body, paying careful attention to his legs and shoulders.

"Ice Lizard?" Linn asked the older Horseman.

Moor nodded, gritting his teeth.

"I'll get some buckets of water to cool you down. I don't think you'll be walking yourself out for a while." Linn stood. A couple of the Chieftain's guards who had rushed toward the commotion volunteered to help Linn.

"Not until I cauterize this arm," Susana said as she tied off the bandage. The healer placed a hand on his shoulder. "You're going to be fine. After you're able to shift shape, it will speed the healing process. You're lucky to have made the flight after losing so much blood, though."

"Where's your Gatherer?" Inez asked, fear twisting her belly.

"Terra took him."

"Terra?" Inez stood, suddenly remembering her husband. Not that she'd really forgotten him. She'd just been so concerned with Moor that for a moment she hadn't thought straight.

Wings beat over the Running Way and she saw Terra's glistening black body and four white feet cutting through the clouds. In spite of the apparent burden of two men and cargo, his landing was classic. As she ran toward him, the men slipped off his back. Dav instantly unbuckled the girth on his saddle as the two men hurried to unload it.

Gods, he looked tired! His ears were pinned and his man's chest heaved. Leaning forward, he braced his hands against his equine front. Sweat ran like rain down his entire body.

He straightened, his bloodshot gaze fixing on Inez as he pulled off his harness.

"I heard what happened," Inez said when he started to explain. "Just catch your breath first. You can tell me more later."

She took the wet harness from him and began helping the men unload the cargo and take off the saddle. There was no time to waste. Terra needed to cool down fast, she realized, placing a hand to his pulsing side, feeling the distended veins beneath his drenched coat.

She noted his breathing had already begun to slow and he neither wheezed nor coughed. Few Horsemen could have traveled such a distance, overburdened, and held up as well as Terra. His legs and body stood strong, no tell-tale wobbling for him.

"How's Moor?" Terra asked.

"Susana's caring for him. She said he'll be fine," Inez told him.

"He's alive," Moor's Gatherer said as he dropped Rock Blood in a half-full sack. "So am I, thanks to you."

"I did my job. Same as you and Moor would have done."

"Well, I'm proud to work with you," the Gatherer stated.

"So am I," Dav added, taking the saddle and blanket from Terra's back. "That's it. I'll take care of the tack for you. Go to the lake or something."

"That's where I'm headed," Terra said, grasping Inez's hand, as they left the Running Way. His palm and fingers felt so hot and his hand trembled slightly from exertion. Still, he wore a cocky look in his red-tinged eyes as he offered her a grin and said, "So how was your night?"

"Oh, Terra!" She couldn't keep from smiling. "I love you. I really love you."

The sound of hoofbeats to her right drew her attention to Kraig who stood, his reddish full-coat lathered from the journey, glaring at Terra. Terra met his gaze, his expression disgusted, before he turned his attention back to Inez.

"What's wrong with him?" She tilted her head in Kraig's direction.

"He's a lazy son-of-a-bitch, that's what's wrong with him. He could have carried that rider part of the way, not that he had to. He's the only one of the party who didn't offer any kind of assistance. I'm sending a message to General Sota. I want him the hell out of this village. Anyone, Horseman or human, who can't be depended on during a Gathering is useless."

"I agree. And he's so jealous of you he reeks of it."

"I don't know what his problem is, but I'm through dealing with him."

* * * * *

Casper curled his lip in revulsion as he approached Kraig, who kicked his back hooves so hard against a thick old oak tree that the trunk dented and the ground shook. The Horseman's coat was frothy from his flight. Nothing looked more disgusting than a sweaty, stinking Horseman in full-coat.

"Bastard!" Kraig muttered under his breath.

"I take it you're referring to the hero of the hour, the magnificent Terra," Casper said.

"Hero of the hour," Kraig snarled. "He'll do whatever he can to prove what a great Fighting Carrier he is, even carry two useless humans on his back for a Spikeland journey!"

"Yes. And he seems to have done it well." Casper tapped his booted foot against the same tree Kraig had kicked.

Kraig growled, his hairy fists clenching and his teeth grinding. "You expect us to find a moment of weakness in *him*. That's your plan? Good luck! His equine-half is more ox-like!"

"If you're so eager to prove yourself, why didn't you offer to carry the second rider for part of the journey?"

Kraig's green eyes gleamed with rage. "Do I look like a fool? I'm not going to risk bursting my lungs and breaking my back for a fucking human. For profit, maybe, but not for one of *your* kind."

"I told you we must bide our time. The chance to strike will come, and the mighty Terra will fall to his knotted equine knees."

"You better be right," Kraig said. "Or else I'm bearing the closeness of your human stench for nothing."

"Not for nothing. I have another proposition for you."

"What now?"

"How would you like the chance to earn a good deal of extra coin?"

"I already work enough."

"But you don't make much profit as a Fighting Carrier. Even the private Carriers and Gatherers pay a portion of their wages to whatever village supports them. This will be coin clear and clean for us to split."

Kraig wore a disgusted expression, but interest flickered in his eyes. "What do you propose?"

"The Gathering season is almost over. Soon there will be few Carriers and Gatherers left in the villages around here. They'll either be visiting family and friends during their time off, or looking for extra work on the tropical islands."

"Tell me something I don't know, human."

"The storage houses will be full and the guard will be down for the winter months. After all, what excitement ever happens in winter? Everyone's hibernating in their homes. There are fewer guards on the storage houses —"

Kraig grinned. "I believe I know what you're suggesting."

"There are some traders I know who'd pay top dollar to have some extra Rock Blood to sell to wealthy people hoarding up private supplies. Are you interested?"

"We'll see."

"Think about it, Horseman. It will be worth your while."

Chapter Seven
Wild Horses

It took Terra over an hour to completely cool down after the flight. After he shifted to Huform, he and Inez stopped at the longhouse to see Moor. Susana told them he was asleep and fairly comfortable.

As Inez and Terra walked hand in hand to their cottage, she noted his pace was a bit slower than usual. She knew that while shape changing encouraged rapid healing, the effects of severe injuries or even tremendous physical exertion could still be felt by Horsemen in their Huform. She didn't doubt Terra had some aching muscles and general fatigue after tonight's flight. When she'd rubbed him down, she'd taken extra care with his legs.

"When we get home I'll give you another massage," she said.

"That sounds so good, but I'm afraid I might be a little disappointing. I'm really ready for some sleep."

"I meant I'd massage you to sleep. Nothing else." She squeezed his hand tighter. "I'm so proud of you, Terra, and so grateful. It would have been horrible to lose Moor. He's been like a father to me since my own family died."

"You grew up with him?"

"Yes."

"I didn't know that."

"I don't talk much about my past. It wasn't very happy."

"I understand." He slipped his hand from hers to caress her nape. "Someday you might talk to me about it. You can tell me anything, you know."

She gazed up at him. "I know. I always feel so safe with you, Terra."

"I'm glad."

They'd nearly reached the house when she spoke again. "My parents died from the Plague. They were both healers and had volunteered in a poor village with not enough Rock Blood to supply everyone. I caught the Plague, too, but I survived. Moor was among the first group of Fighting Carriers to fully supply the village. You Fighting Carriers aren't like most of the people in private business. Your duty is to help people and keep up supplies, even when you make little or no profit. Most of you are good men."

"Wait, wait. Moor was a Fighting Carrier?"

She nodded. "Don't say I told you. He doesn't like talking about it."

"Why?"

"His wife died while he was on a Gathering. The Fighting Carrier in charge of his party knew a message had been sent, telling Moor to come quickly if he wanted to see his wife before she died. The Horseman didn't give him the message until he returned from the Gathering. By the time he arrived at his home village, it was too late."

"He blamed the Fighting Carriers because he couldn't be with her. I understand how he must feel. If anything were to happen to you, it would kill me not to be with you."

"His wife also shared dreams with him."

Terra's brow furrowed. "How sad."

"His trip to our village was his last as a Fighting Carrier. He hired himself out to private Gatherings after that. And he took care of me. I think we felt some sort of kinship, with him just losing his wife and me losing my parents. He was the first Horseman I ever rode and he trained me as a Gatherer."

"No wonder you care so much about him."

Inez thought she detected a note of jealousy in his voice.

"I think of him as a father." Inez stared up at him. "You need never worry about any man coming between us, Terra. I belong to you."

"I love you so much, Inez."

"Oh Terra, tonight when I'd heard someone had been injured, I was so afraid it was you." She threw her arms around him. "Of course I panicked when I saw it was Moor, but my first thought was of you. When I heard you'd carried an extra man, I was terrified you'd damaged yourself."

Laughter rumbled deep in his chest as he held her close. "It would take a hell of a lot more than that to damage me. I've done just about everything during my time with the Fighting Carriers. I'm a rugged ol' Horseman, my love."

"I was worried because I know you'd hurt yourself before dropping a human to their death, just like Moor."

"That's what his rider said about him, not that the rest of us couldn't tell by how he struggled. I can definitely see how he was a Fighting Carrier."

They'd reached their cottage and stepped inside. While Terra started a fire in the hearth, Inez undressed and turned down their bed.

"Take off your clothes and lie down," she said.

He did as she asked. Once he'd stretched out on his stomach, Inez knelt beside him, kneading his shoulders and back. His thick muscles felt tense as she rubbed them in soothing, circular motions until he relaxed beneath her.

"Feels good," he murmured, half asleep.

She kissed his cheek before continuing the massage, pressing the heels of her palms into his waist and the small of his back. He uttered a soft moan when she caressed his Turning Point, but she didn't spend much time there. Her goal was to relax, not stimulate. She rubbed his buttocks, thighs, calves and feet. By the time she'd finished, he was deeply asleep. Inez curled up beside him, covering them both with a sheet. Even in cool weather, a heavy blanket wasn't necessary when sleeping beside a Horseman. Their body temperature was far higher than a human's. All that heat felt so good, especially in the wintertime.

"Good night, Terra," she whispered, taking a tendril of his curly black hair between her fingers and kissing it. "I love you."

* * * * *

The following afternoon, Inez and Terra stood in the tack house preparing for their last flight before the Gatherings finally stopped for winter.

Moor, in Huform, his arm still bandaged, joined them as Inez wrapped Terra's back legs with bandages while he wrapped his front ones. She knew his muscles were probably a little sore after last night's flight, and the bandages would provide added protection during the journey.

"I can't thank you enough for what you did," Moor said. "I was fine until the damn arm started bleeding again. I kept tying it up, but it's not easy to do a field dressing in mid-flight."

"Like I said, you'd have done the same for me."

"We had a good team yesterday. Almost everyone pulled together, and I'm grateful to each of you who did."

"It's all right, Moor. I know who you're talking about." Terra straightened and fastened his harness. "Kraig has flown his last Gathering with any of my parties."

"He gives a bad name to Fighting Carriers, but there's always an element of Horseman who joins simply for the prestige of being elite."

"That prestige has been earned by some of the finest Horsemen in our history. A man who can't pull together with his party has no place among them. I've known private Carriers with far more integrity."

"Present company included, I hope." Moor grinned.

"Without a doubt."

"I'm just glad you're feeling better, Moor." Inez slipped her arms around her friend in an uncharacteristic display of affection.

Moor squeezed her tightly. "You've got yourself a good Horseman, Inez. I couldn't have hoped for better for you."

"Are you leaving today?" she asked.

"After you get back." Moor glanced at Terra and shrugged. "She's like a daughter to me. I need to know she's back safely before I can go anywhere. Even though I should be going on this Gathering, if it wasn't for the damn injury. Makes me feel so useless."

"We all have to rest up at one time or another," Terra said. "Enjoy your time off."

"Your brother will be glad to see you." Inez told Moor. "You haven't visited him and his family in a while."

Moor followed them outside where Inez mounted. She waved to Moor who called, "Safe journey!"

Before stepping onto the Running Way, Terra waited for Linn and his Gatherer to take to the sky.

"Ready, my love?" Terra asked when the path was free.

"Whenever you are."

He picked up to a gallop and, wings beating, ascended.

"Just think about all the time we'll have to play this winter!" Inez called.

"And the bathhouse is just about finished! It will be a pleasure on snowy days—and nights!"

She rubbed between his shoulder blades. "I can hardly wait!"

* * * * *

The Gathering went smoothly, though the flight home was a bit rough due to the direction of the winds. They'd received notice a few days ago from Horsemen scouts sent to check the islands that the Spikes had begun covering several of the western islands. Others would soon be covered as well, then not even scouts would fly out again until the spring.

Inez was glad for some time off for her and her new husband. Perhaps they could start working seriously on those children Terra wanted so much. To her surprise, she longed for them, too. A human daughter and hopefully a Horseman son. She hoped they'd inherit Terra's beautiful mouth rather than her homely one, even though he said he hoped they looked exactly like her.

They arrived home after dark and were greeted by Moor and Susana who came to the track to meet Linn.

Inez felt a wave of deja vu as Susana gazed up at Linn and asked, "Would you like company while you cool down?"

The young Horseman smiled broadly and took her hand in his hair-covered one. They began circling the outside edge of the Running Way. Apparently Susana appreciated Linn's full-coat as much as Inez liked Terra's.

Less than an hour later, Inez and Terra were on their way home. It might have been the way Terra swept her into his arms, carried her inside and nearly ripped off all her clothes, but she knew he was quite in the mood for lovemaking.

When she was naked, he placed her on a stool against the wall. He tore off his clothes then pressed his warm, naked body to hers.

"Just think," he said, "if we want we can make love all night and sleep all day."

"Did you plan on it?"

"What do you think?" He kissed his way down her breasts and belly until he reached her soft mound.

Kneeling before her, he licked her pussy and clit, sucking the tender little nub. Inez closed her eyes and leaned against the wall, her hands playing with his thick, curly hair. He knew her body well enough to sense when she was about to explode and stopped licking as she teetered on the edge of orgasm.

Standing, he thrust into her, squeezing her buttocks and lifting her. She locked her legs around his waist and clung to him as he thrust. It took only a few strokes before she quivered and throbbed in orgasm.

Still hard inside her, he carried her to the bed and placed her on the edge as he knelt, thrusting. Inez moaned, her head sinking into the mattress as her hips thrust in time with his. The next orgasm made her tingle with pleasure from the roots of her hair to the tips of her toes.

He slipped his cock from her and dragged her up the bed. Stretching out beside her, he caressed her breasts and belly with long strokes of his fingertips. Inez moaned, contented, and turned to him. As she edged closer, he slipped an arm around her waist and pulled her against the length of his hard, heated body. The tip of his cock poked against her slick pussy before he entered her again. Side by side, wrapped in each other's arms, they made love slowly, tenderly.

"I love you, Terra," she whispered, stroking his face. Now that she'd admitted it aloud, she couldn't seem to say it enough.

He kissed her forehead and lips while massaging her back. "My heart is yours, Inez."

With legs entwined and their arms tight around one another, their rhythm increased. Inez pressed her face to his shoulder and he buried his in her neck as she throbbed in the marvelous throes of another climax. He came soon after, his taut body stiffening even more as he groaned his pleasure, then relaxed.

Inez pushed herself to her knees and gazed down at Terra, who watched her with flames smoldering behind his relaxed expression. Gods, she wondered if she'd ever grow tired of looking at him. Her fingertips trailed over his hard chest and traced each of his ribs, which appeared more prominent than usual due to the increase in Gatherings. As Spike season neared, most of the Carriers wore down to raw bones and muscle. On a large, perfectly proportioned Horseman like Terra, the weight loss only seemed to make him look sleeker.

She bent, touching her lips to his torso just over his heart. It beat slow and steady. Closing her eyes, she ran the flat of her tongue over one of his nipples before settling onto the bed beside him.

After a moment, Terra stood, pressed a gentle kiss to the top of her head, and strode outside. Thinking he'd gone to relieve himself, Inez stretched and closed her eyes, sighing with contentment as she awaited his return.

Her eyes flew open when she heard the clatter of hooves on the cottage floor. Terra swept her off the bed and held her close to his chest.

"What are you doing?" she giggled, writhing with ticklish pleasure as he licked and kissed her neck.

"I want another flight before we go to sleep."

"Honestly, Terra, sometimes it seems nothing can wear you out!"

"Sometimes I feel nothing can." He wiggled his eyebrows and headed for the door, Inez still snug in his arms. Inez gazed at the star-filled sky as she stroked the strong column of Terra's throat.

"Look at me," he ordered.

She gazed into his eyes, her belly tightening at the burning expression in them. The tip of his tongue moistened his lips. She felt his chest expand as he drew a deep breath. "You know I'll always keep you safe when we're in the sky?"

"Of course." Inez lifted her hand to his cheek.

"Put both arms around my neck and hold on tight."

Without hesitation, she did as he asked, clinging to his neck and burying her face in his shoulder. His arms tightened around her, holding her close as he broke into a run. Inez's heart pounded with excitement as he ascended quickly. Wind struck her, harder than she'd ever felt when behind the protection of his torso. His wings pounded the air, though she knew he was flying much slower than usual.

"All right, let go of my neck," he said.

"You must be joking!" She wasn't about to let go of him when they were so high.

"I won't drop you. I promise."

Slowly, Inez released her grip on him, nearly panicking when he began turning her in his arms. "What are you doing!"

He molded her body to his, one arm wrapped firmly around her middle. "Now reach up and hold me."

Her breathing shallow, Inez extended her arms over her head and grasped the sides of Terra's neck with both hands.

"Now relax," he said.

"In this position?"

He chuckled, his chest vibrating beneath her back. She had to admit that being pinned close to Terra's man-chest offered her a point of view she'd never imagined possible. This had to be as close as a human could get to experiencing flight through a Horseman's eyes.

Terra's free arm slipped down Inez's body. His fingers stroked the triangle of hair between her legs. Inez shivered as much from the chill of the night wind as from lust, as he began fondling her clit and pussy. Inez moaned, her buttocks rubbing against his body, loving the feel of his warm human skin on his man's torso and the sleek coat covering his equine chest. His fingers, slick with love syrup gathered from her aching pussy, rubbed first one side of her clit then the other. The hand moved upward, cupping one of her breasts while his thumb rubbed her nipple.

"This is amazing!" Inez breathed, tilting her head against him, her eyes half closed against the wind. She gasped when he reached between her legs again, his middle finger swirling inside her while his thumb stroked her clit. "Oh! Terra! Oh yes, love! Yes!"

The thought of attaining orgasm while helplessly suspended so far above ground pushed Inez's passion to its limits. A few more strokes of Terra's deft fingers and she shattered, her hot, throbbing pussy gripping his still-probing finger as her clit ached and pulsed to the stroking of his thumb.

As Inez recovered, she became aware of his heart slamming against her back and his neck throbbing beneath her palms. She knew his ragged breathing had nothing to do with the short, slow flight, but with a buildup of sexual tension.

"Gods, I want you so badly!" he said in a raw voice.

"Then bring me home and take me."

Making a wide turn, he slipped an arm beneath her legs and moved his other around her back, once again holding her in a normal fashion.

"Aren't I getting heavy?" she asked. "Your arms must be killing you."

"You hardly seem to weigh anything at all."

"How can you stand the wind when you fly?" She buried her face in his chest as a particularly strong gust sent a shiver through her entire body.

"It's what Horsemen are built for."

"That and other things." She grinned.

Growling with desire, he returned her smile, squeezing her tighter as he glided to a landing in the field behind their cottage.

* * * * *

The next morning, after bathing and breakfast, Inez and Terra packed a basket of food for their afternoon meal and decided on a walk in the meadows several miles from the village.

Terra kept his Huform as they strolled side-by-side, discussing pleasant and trivial matters.

"You've never told me about your family." She glanced at him as they walked.

A faint smile tilted up the corners of Terra's finely-shaped lips. "You'd have liked my parents. My father was a Fighting Carrier—one of the best. He flew thousands of Gatherings in his time."

She grinned. "I see where you've gotten your heart from, then."

"He was a tough old Horseman, that's for sure. He died on a Gathering the year I joined the Fighting Carriers."

Inez squeezed his hand tighter. "I'm so sorry."

"I am too, but he died doing what he loved more than anything else. The old man was born to fly, there was no doubt about that."

"And your mother?"

"She was a good woman and very pretty, but what son doesn't think his mother's pretty, I suppose. She died a couple of days after giving birth to my sister."

"I didn't know you had a sister."

"I want to visit her with you sometime this winter. I sent her a message about moving here before I left the Hall of Fighting Carriers, but she hasn't answered yet. She's a messenger and has probably been away delivering other people's news."

"Interesting work for a woman."

"She's a stubborn girl. Didn't want to be dependent on anyone after our father died. I'm sure you'll like her."

"From the sound of it, I think I already do."

Pounding hooves interrupted their conversation. A small herd of wild true-horses cantered to the crest of the nearest hill. They paused before spreading over the field, their graceful necks arched as they fed on the tender grass.

"Nice animals," Terra observed.

Inez giggled.

He glanced at her. "What?"

"There's something I've heard about Horsemen and have often wondered."

Terra smiled. "Here it comes."

"You know?"

"I can only guess. Go ahead and ask anyway. I might be wrong."

"Do Horsemen ever...you know...take their pleasure with true-horses?"

He laughed, tilting his handsome face skyward. "I knew it! Humans invariably ask that question."

"Well?"

He held her eyes. "Can you picture *me* making love with a horse? Yes, there are some perverted Horsemen who screw true-horses, just as there are some perverted humans who screw sheep—or so I've heard. Inez, to a normal, rational Horseman, making love with a true-horse would be akin to a human making love with an ape."

"Sorry." She blushed. "I didn't think you would, but I'd heard stories."

"I guess I can't blame you for curiosity, but it seems I'll have to double my efforts when I make love with you," he teased, yanking her into his arms and covering her neck with kisses. "I don't want my wife wondering what kind of female I want to make love with."

"I didn't mean you, Terra!" She giggled as he pressed his lips to her neck and blew, the sensation tickling her to her toes.

He released her, and they decided to eat their meal under an apple tree on a nearby hill, so they could watch the horses.

Though wild, this particular herd wasn't unfamiliar to Inez. She recognized the five chestnut mares and the big brown stallion. They knew her as well and had learned to trust her so much that she'd actually ridden several of the mares bareback. She grinned. Riding Terra bareback was nothing like riding a true-horse.

"Have you ever ridden a true-horse, Terra? In your Huform, of course."

"Hell yes," he said, taking a chunk of bread from the basket and splitting it with her. "Horses are wonderful. They like people, too, and they're rarely afraid of Horsemen, even in our Huform."

"I wasn't sure if a Horseman would be bothered riding a true-horse, since your speed and endurance far surpasses theirs."

"It's more enjoyment of sharing friendship with such a primitive animal. Truth be told, I wouldn't mind a ride on that stallion, if he'll let me. Most wild true-horses are too small for me to ride, but this group is unusually large for these parts."

"I think they came up from the west where the horses are bigger."

"Most likely."

When they finished the meal, Inez and Terra approached the herd slowly. Several of the mares as well as the stallion lifted their elongated heads and stared at them. The stallion stamped one of his massive hooves and his ears twitched. Inez knew he recognized her. Though he didn't know Terra, the Horseman's scent didn't frighten him as would a strange human's.

"You going to run from me, big boy?" Terra spoke softly to the stallion as he stepped closer, extending his hand.

Inez's gaze switched from the horse to Terra, her heart pounding with anticipation. The excitement of gaining the trust of wild horses was still something she enjoyed.

The stallion stood his ground as Terra approached, allowing the Horseman to touch his neck. The animal quivered, his eyes flashing, before he turned and galloped away. Terra chased, his long legs swallowing ground. Even in Huform, Horsemen were much faster than humans, about as fast as a true-horse. Terra reached the stallion, sliding his arms around his neck and swinging onto his back. The stallion bucked twice, then continued his gallop, his dark hooves sending chunks of grass flying as he raced.

The mares watched their leader with the man on his back. The one closest to Inez whinnied. Inez approached, murmuring softly. Eventually the mare allowed Inez to stroke her neck and shoulder.

Inez watched as Terra used his hands and knees to guide the stallion back to the herd. She knew anyone but a Horseman would never have gotten close enough to the stallion to touch him, let alone ride him. The stallion stopped, scarcely winded from the short run, and Terra slipped off his back. The horse nudged Terra's shoulder in an almost affectionate gesture before trotting away to continue standing watch over his herd.

Terra approached Inez and the mare. He stroked the horse's nose before taking Inez's hand. Together they gathered the remains of their meal and packed it into the basket.

They walked over two more hills until they reached the lake.

"Mind if I swim?" Terra asked, removing his shirt.

"Go ahead. It's too cold for me." Inez settled under another tree and faced the lake. She watched, sighing with pleasure, as Terra removed his trousers. The sculpted muscles of his Huform rippled across his back, buttocks and legs as he stepped into the lake. When the water reached his chest, she watched him close his eyes and shudder, sending ripples through the lake's surface. He'd changed shape, of that she was certain. Though he'd never let her see his lower half when it happened, she had recognized the other signs of his shifting.

He emerged from the water on four sturdy legs and approached her. Lying down beside her, he rested his head in her lap while she stroked his thick black curls, wet from the lake.

"I'll carry you home," Terra said, "as soon as I dry off. I don't want to make you cold."

Inez sighed, uttering a contented sound, as she leaned her head back against the tree and closed her eyes. Though she felt the days had grown too cold for swimming, they were still pleasant for sitting outside. With the sun beating down, the feeling of Terra so close and the idea they had the winter free of Gatherings, she relaxed enough to fall into a light sleep.

She awoke to Terra's mouth brushing hers with a kiss.

Her eyes flickered open and she slipped her arms around his neck, hugging him tightly.

"I suppose we should get home," Inez said. "Susana and Linn are joining us for supper tonight. I want to prepare something special."

"Good. Linn said he'll be staying in the village for the winter. He and I will be the only Horsemen here until the new Gathering season starts, aside from Moor, that is, when he returns in a few weeks. I wonder how much of an influence Susana had over Linn's staying?" Terra's eyes gleamed with amusement.

Inez laughed as she mounted Terra. "Hmmm, I wonder."

With Terra carrying her, it took only minutes for them to reach the cottage. While Inez went inside to prepare her famous stew recipe, Terra changed back to Huform outside. Horsemen could safely change without preparation, provided their muscles weren't overused and their bodies overheated, so within moments he stepped inside.

Inez glanced at him from where she adjusted the stew pot over the fire. "I'll be a few minutes, then I'll leave it to simmer and we can do other things."

"Oh, I plan on it." Terra's voice carried a seductive edge as he held up two long black feathers he'd obviously plucked from his wings before changing shape.

He stepped close to her and ran the feathers over her cheeks and down her nose. They felt soft yet incredibly arousing. Her belly tightened as she considered what they'd feel like tickling her entire body. Was that what he had in mind?

Inez hurried to prepare the stew while Terra turned down the sheets on the bed. Watching him walk around the house naked was an incredible distraction, but somehow Inez managed to finish chopping all the ingredients and set the stew to cooking over the fire. She washed her hands, dried them, and undressed. Terra stared at her as she first removed her boots, her trousers, and last her shirt. She unbraided her hair and shook it out so it hung thick and dark down her shoulders.

"Come, Inez. Lie on your back." He leaned against the wall by the bed, one impossibly long, sleekly-muscled leg crossed over the other, his arms folded over his thick, hair-roughened chest, the feathers twitching in his grasp, brushing his bulging biceps.

She trembled with anticipation as she did as he ordered.

"Close your eyes," he said.

She did, her breathing already increased and her heart throbbing. She shivered at the first touch of a feather across her brow. The tip moved down her nose and over her cheeks while the second feather danced across her breasts. He used a feather to stroke both of her nipples at once. Inez's belly clenched and she felt her pussy turning to liquid. Oh Gods, this was too good!

The feathers swept her belly, the tip of one dipping into her navel before tracing the edge of her pubic hair. She felt feathers running along the joining of her thighs and pelvis. Soft strokes brushed down her legs. She jerked and giggled when one of the feathers tickled the bottom of her feet.

His warm, callused hands parted her thighs, and the feather dipped between her legs. The soft tip, now moist with her juices, tickled her clit.

"Oh Terra!" she cried, her neck arching into the pillow as he continued stroking her clit with the feather. The touch was so arousing yet elusive. Her pulse throbbed and her body felt as hot as a Horseman's after a Gathering. The feather was suddenly replaced by Terra's lips and tongue. He held her by the waist as she dug her fingers into his scalp and moaned uncontrollably. Her legs shook as they slipped over his shoulders and she came longer and harder than she ever had in her life.

Chapter Eight
In the Tropics

By the end of the week, all the Horsemen except for Terra, Linn and Kraig, as well as most of the Gatherers, had left Hornview for the winter. Inez always thought it was strange in the wintertime, with the village half empty. Usually, she and Moor were the only Gathering members remaining, and occasionally they would leave for a few weeks to visit his brother's family.

This winter would be different, though. She had Terra. And Susana had Linn, though the couple hadn't admitted to a formal courtship. Yet. Inez had no doubts it wouldn't be long.

The four often shared meals together and talked about next year's Gathering season.

"I don't know what's been going on," Susana said one evening when she and Linn ate supper at Inez and Terra's cottage. "There seems to be a leak in the Rock Blood supply. I've split open a few stones and they're dry."

Terra's eyes narrowed. "Unusual. They all felt full when we carried them, I can guarantee that."

"Sounds like thievery to me," Linn added.

"I wouldn't doubt it." Terra nodded in the youth's direction. "We can check the supply houses ourselves after we eat."

"Casper is already taking care of it," Susana said. "I went to the Chieftain right away and he told Casper to find out what the problem is."

Terra and Inez exchanged glances. Though Casper was the Captain of the Guard and in charge of village security, neither liked nor trusted him. Not that he hadn't always performed his job well, and the Chieftain favored him greatly.

"It still can't hurt for us to take a look," Terra said. "After all, it was our backs that carried the supplies, not those of Casper and his guards."

"I agree," Linn said. "And another thing, I don't like how Kraig has stayed on, even after those issues with the Fighting Carriers."

Terra, ordering Kraig to accompany him, had traveled back to the Hall of Fighting Carriers a few days after the near-fatal Gathering with Moor. He'd demanded that Kraig be removed from Hornview, and General Sota had complied. Kraig, in a fit of rage, denounced the Fighting Carriers and withdrew his service. He'd since become a private Carrier and solicited Hornview's Chieftain who, with encouragement from Casper, hired him to join the village's personal Gathering Parties.

Both Terra and Linn had been furious, not to mention Dav and Moor's Gatherer. Other Gatherers refused to ride Kraig, so he was often used as a Rock Blood Carrier and fighter only on Gatherings. Though such a position was considered insulting, Kraig seemed to prefer it. His distaste for humans was obvious in his words and actions, and both Inez and Terra wondered why he'd chosen to remain among humans over the off-season.

"He's trouble," Inez stated. "I don't like him."

"You and most of the village. Only Casper and the Chieftain seem satisfied with him because he carries enormous supplies of Rock Blood. That Horseman is all business and only seems to care about wealth." Susana looked disgusted.

"Well that's not why I became a Fighting Carrier," Linn said. "And I'm glad he left. Everyone knows the only way to become rich is by Gathering for private business."

"Let's not talk anymore about greedy Chieftains, Carriers and guards," Susana said. "I've brought a honey-raisin cake for dessert, and I'm dying to eat it with happy thoughts."

"Sounds good to me." Linn smiled.

Terra licked his lips. "I'm all for cake. Inez?"

"You have to ask?" Inez stood to help Susana slice the cake and prepare tea. Before she walked away, Terra affectionately slapped her buttocks. She grinned over her shoulder at him and thought what a wonderful winter it was going to be.

* * * * *

It was less than two weeks after the season ended when a disappointing message arrived, its contents only softened by the knowledge that Terra's sister delivered it.

It was noon and Terra and Inez were walking around the Running Way after an exercise flight when a black-haired woman on a tall black stallion thundered into the village square.

"Eh, it's Phillipa!" Terra grinned. "Come on."

He gave Inez an arm onto his still-warm back and trotted to the longhouse where his sister had dismounted from the blowing stallion. She glanced in their direction as she began walking her horse out.

"Terra!" She smiled, waving. Inez noted Phillipa looked much like her brother, very tall with large blue eyes and a square jaw. Her lean, big-boned body moved gracefully as she and her horse walked toward them.

"I got the chance to bring some messages to Hornview and I had to take it." Phillipa accepted a powerful hug from Terra. "I wanted to see my brother and his new wife." She turned her gaze to Inez. "Am I right in guessing you're Inez?"

"Yes. It's good to meet you, Phillipa." Inez accepted the woman's firm handshake.

"Oh!" Phillipa reached into the leather bag slung across her shoulder and withdrew a slip of parchment. "One of the messages is for you, Terra."

Inez glanced over Terra's shoulder as he held the message up for both of them to read. Inez's belly sank. The message was from a Fighting Carrier in a village several hundred miles south of Hornview. He was in charge of Gathering Parties to the tropics, but had a badly sprained leg and needed reinforcements until General Sota dispatched a replacement for him. From the message, the village was small with few Carriers, though due to an outbreak of Plague nearby, Horsemen were forced to make several trips a day.

"Do you know where I can find a Horseman called Linn?" Phillipa asked. "I have a message for him, too."

"He's in the longhouse," Inez said.

"Would you take my horse for a few minutes, since it looks like you're cooling down too? I'll deliver this message and be right back."

Terra took the stallion's reins and headed toward the Running Way.

"He's probably been asked to cover someone as well." Terra glanced over his shoulder at Inez. She hoped she didn't look quite as disappointed as she felt.

"I'll only be gone a week, maybe less. General Sota will send a replacement fast."

"Can I go with you?"

Terra wrinkled his nose. "The tropics are horrible, and from the letter, the trips are intense."

"You know that won't bother me."

"I know, but with the Plague around those parts, I don't want to risk you catching it, even if there is enough Rock Blood to go around. I want you to stay here, Inez."

Inez's stomach clenched as she slipped off his back and took the stallion's reins from him, stroking the horse's sweaty neck as they walked alongside Terra. Was it beginning? The part of marriage in which the husband issued orders to the wife? She wanted none of it. "I don't like being told what to do, Terra. I won't be told what to do!"

"I've never tried to control you, Inez. I want you to do this for me because I love you and it will ease my mind knowing you're safe in Hornview."

Inez stared into his wide blue eyes. Frustration still twisted her gut, but to her dismay, it melted when faced with his tender words. Damn him! "All right, Terra. I'll stay here. But you hurry home — safely, of course."

"Of course." He bent and brushed her cheek with a kiss.

"The bathhouse will probably be done by the time you get back." She scratched his chest with her fingertips. "I can't wait for us to test it out together."

"Umm," he growled deep in his chest, "neither can I."

"Terra!" Linn called as he walked across the Running Way in his Huform, Susana and Phillipa beside him.

"Where have you been sent?" Terra asked.

"Back to the Hall. They need an assistant trainer to fill in for a few weeks with the new recruits." Linn couldn't keep the proud gleam from his eyes.

"You'll do well," Terra said. "I have no doubt."

"Thank you. I couldn't have done any of this without your training."

"I might have helped, but your talent and drive come from within. Heart is something no one can give you. You're either born with it or you're not."

"That's true," Phillipa said, taking her horse's reins from Inez. "I might not be a shapeshifter, but I'm still a Horseman's daughter. They don't ask just any Fighting Carrier to train recruits, Linn."

"I know you'll be a great trainer." Susana gazed up at Linn. "I'm going to miss you, though."

"I'll miss you, too." The young Carrier wrapped an arm around Susana's waist and covered her mouth with a tender kiss that left both of them blushing.

"Sorry," Linn murmured, his eyes still fixed on Susana's. "I guess a Running Way isn't the best place for a first kiss."

"It's fine with me," Susana breathed, unable to take her eyes from him.

Inez and Terra exchanged smiles as they glanced at the couple walking back to the longhouse.

"There's nothing like love," Terra admitted.

"Nothing in the world."

"So I've heard," Phillipa said, her tone sarcastic. "I wouldn't know. I don't think love's for me."

"That's what I thought," Inez said.

"Well, I have to finish cooling off Black Silk." Phillipa patted her stallion's neck. "Then we'll find a place to camp out for the night."

"Camp out? Come to our house," Inez said.

"You don't mind?"

"Yes, we mind," Terra teased. "There's no room for my only blood relative left."

"Well, if you put it that way, I'll be glad to." Phillipa grinned.

* * * * *

Unfortunately, both Terra and Linn had to leave for their duties that day. Inez and Phillipa spent the rest of the afternoon in the village with Susana then all three women ate dinner at the longhouse.

"Who, in beauty's name, is this?" Casper said as he swaggered into the longhouse and approached Phillipa. His eyes raked her stunning face and full, firm breasts, the cleavage visible beneath the open ties of her billowy black shirt.

Phillipa raised an eyebrow in disgust and continued her conversation with the others at the table.

"Allow me to introduce myself," Casper continued, practically knocking Susana off the end of the bench as he squeezed in beside Phillipa. "I'm Casper, Captain of the Guard."

Phillipa flung him a sarcastic look. "Congratulations."

"Such sharp tones from a delicate..." Casper's voice faded as Phillipa stood, all six feet one inch of her glowering down at him. "Delicate and tall. Very tall."

"I've heard about you, Casper." Phillipa's disinterested expression suddenly turned warm.

Inez smiled inwardly. This was to be a performance worth watching.

"You don't like Horsemen, right?" Phillipa melted back onto the bench, edging closer to Casper.

"So you *have* heard of me. You know I don't believe a lovely woman like yourself should be forced to bear the beasts' children."

"Oh, I see. Horsemen are brutes, correct?"

"Worse than brutes. Filthy animals. Most of us only tolerate them for the sake of Rock Blood."

"And most of them tolerate you out of appreciation for human females."

"What?" Casper's lip curled.

"Human males are useless. When Horsemen and human females mate, they produce shapeshifting males and human females, so as you can see, you are worthless to both parties."

Casper's teeth gritted. "So you're one of those Horsemen lovers?"

"I'm Terra's sister." Phillipa snarled.

"You're half Horseman?" Casper stood, slinking away from her.

"Proudly. Now get away from me before I vomit from your stench so close to my superior Horseman senses."

Susana laughed and Inez flung Casper a wicked grin as he left the table, cursing to himself.

"To think he wanted to marry you," Phillipa said to Inez. "The idea of it makes my flesh crawl."

"Mine, too," Inez told her.

"Well, that was a beautiful sight." Susana smiled. "I only wish Linn and Terra had been here to see it."

"My brother's seen me at work before." Phillipa waved her hand. "He tells me I have my mother's sharp tongue."

"Apparently not a bad thing to inherit," Inez remarked.

Inez found she had much in common with Phillipa. Both enjoyed the freedom and independence of their jobs, a dislike of Casper and a love of Horsemen. But how could Phillipa not appreciate them? Horseman blood flowed in her veins, and it was apparent in her extreme height and powerful, though beautiful, body. She also had a marvelous way with true-horses. They seemed to trust and obey her on sight.

Inez asked Phillipa to remain at the cottage for a while, so they could get to know each other better. Phillipa readily agreed.

At least she wouldn't be as lonely without Terra, and she hoped Phillipa could stay long enough so her brother could visit with her when he returned from the south.

* * * * *

Nearly a week after he'd received the message from the southern village, Terra was on his way home. General

Sota had sent two Fighting Carriers rather than one, having heard about the difficulties prevailing at that particular village. Terra had to admit it was one of the more problematic missions he'd had. The outbreak of Plague had been severe, depleting most of the Rock Blood. Daily Gatherings were necessary just to keep the humans alive. The strongest Carriers were forced to make several trips a day to harvest enough Rock Blood for storage. When the village's only other large Carrier developed breathing difficulty and was forced to rest, Terra pushed his own limits on the number of Gatherings he flew per day. He knew it was a pace he couldn't keep for long, but he wouldn't need to. The other Carrier was healing well, and reinforcements would come soon. He was grateful when they arrived that morning, and wasted no time in leaving for home. Late last night, he and his party had returned from the worst Gathering yet. One of the Carriers had become ill in flight and dropped precariously close to the sea. The man-eating plants had stretched up their vicious leaves and wrapped around the ailing Horseman and his Gatherer. The rest of the party had risked their own lives flying in to assist, but they were too late. The Horseman and rider were dragged below and devoured. One of the plants had wrapped around Terra's neck when he'd hovered low as his rider attempted to pull the dying Carrier's rider onto Terra's back. Terra's breath was cut off while he beat his wings hard and he and his rider used their swords to slash at the plant until it finally let go.

Touching a hand to his throat, Terra shook his head at the memory as he glided across the sky toward home. Death had been too close last night, and the thought that hurt most was that he wouldn't have gotten to say goodbye to Inez.

Several miles from home, Terra floated to a landing and began walking. Even without mishap, the tropical flights were torturous. The severe heat in those parts was enough to kill humans, let alone Horsemen with their naturally hot bodies. No Horsemen in the tropics used their full-coat, though they smeared their bodies with an herbal paste to protect their skin from the scalding sun. The paste needed to be reapplied often, since it was quickly sweated off. While stationed in southern villages years before, Terra had seen many Horsemen as well as humans suffer from dehydration and severe overheating. It seemed whether Gatherings took place in the north or the south, Carriers and Gatherers took risks.

That's part of the excitement, Terra told himself as he walked slowly down the dirt road leading to Hornview. Flying the rest of the way home would have been faster, but so many journeys in such heat had sapped his strength. He might have rested a day before traveling, but he was eager to see Inez. Besides, the slow walk felt good. Still, he would feel even better with his wife snug in his arms as they curled up for a nap in their bed.

* * * * *

"Kraig, are you alone in here?" Casper asked as he stepped into the tack room.

The redheaded Horseman glanced over his shoulder from where he stood polishing his saddle. "Who the hell else would be here? I'm the only Horseman left in this stinking village, remember?"

"It's time to put our plan in action."

Kraig raised an eyebrow.

Casper continued, "I was out patrolling the surrounding area with my guards and I saw Terra on his way home."

"So?"

"He's walking in." Casper grinned. "Slow."

A smile tugged at Kraig's lips. "It's the tropics. From what I heard, his station was badly overworked. All that heat and little rest is enough to kill a Carrier."

"My thoughts exactly."

"Where's his wife?"

Casper's chest expanded with a deep breath and his eyes gleamed. "With that fucking sister-in-law of hers gone on another delivery and the workers finished with the bathhouse, she's alone at her cottage, except for Susana mixing her potions there. You know how useless healers are when it comes to fighting, so Inez may as well be alone. You can take care of her, and I'll send Terra on the flight to his death."

"I'll take care of her, but I'm not leaving right away. I'll hide her in the cave I've been using to meet with the Rock Blood traders. I'm about to make a very profitable deal for us, but I need to talk with them today."

"That's fine. You'll have time. It will take Terra a couple of hours to fly back to the tropics. When he realizes I've sent him on a false chase, he'll be back. That's another few hours."

Kraig laughed. "By then he'll be so tired he won't be able to catch me if I fly her off to the Spikelands right in front of him."

Casper narrowed his eyes. "Don't get too cocky. You want to make sure you give yourself a good enough head start just in case."

"Like I said, he might be half ox, but he's no god. We all have our limits, human. Our plan will ensure his death—and hers."

* * * * *

The sound of beating wings outside the cottage sent Inez's heart fluttering.

"Terra!" She smiled, dropping her broom and rushing outside. Susana, who had been visiting with her, followed.

Inez' belly tightened when Kraig strode from the side of the house.

"What do you want?" she demanded.

"Just a visit with the wife of my former teacher."

"Get out of here, Kraig. I'm busy." Inez stepped into the house and closed the door. Moments later it flew off its hinges.

Kraig lowered his head as he stepped inside, his hooves clattering on the stone floor.

"Get out of here! Now!" Inez bellowed, slipping her dagger from her boot.

Susana reached for the broom, poking it at Kraig who ripped it from her grasp and used the end to butt her in the stomach. Susana dropped to her knees, grasping her middle.

As Kraig advanced on Inez, she swiped at him. He growled when she slashed at his arm. He half-reared, one of his powerful front hooves knocking the dagger from her hand. She bit his arm and kicked one of his front legs as he wrapped his hand in her hair. The crack of his fist across her face sent her crashing over a chair. Inez's vision blurred as she spat a mouthful of blood from her cut lip, yet she wasted no time springing to her feet.

Susana threw pottery dishes at Kraig. The Horseman laughed as he raised his arms to deflect the blows.

"Get the hell out of here!" Susana shouted.

Inez picked up the chair she'd fallen over and hurled it at Kraig. He glanced over his shoulder in time to kick it with his rear legs before it struck his back.

"Enough of this!" Kraig charged at Inez, his ears pressed close to his head, and yanked her into his arms. She thrust her elbows into his man chest and used her heels to kick at his equine legs. The last thing she remembered was a hard whack in the back of her head. Then everything faded to black.

* * * * *

"Terra!" Casper bellowed as he and his true-horse mounted the crest of the hill on the outskirts of Hornview.

Terra's lip curled. What the hell did he want? The last person he wanted to see was the Captain of the Guard.

Casper galloped to Terra, his expression frantic. "He's taken her!"

"What?" Terra demanded, a knot forming in the pit of his stomach.

"That stinking bastard Kraig! He's taken Inez!"

Terra grasped Casper's arm. Hard. His teeth gritted as he glared into the Captain's wide eyes. "Speak!"

"He'd been talking about picking up some extra work with the slavers on Blanchard Isle, but I didn't think he meant to use our women here."

Terra's pulse raced. Damn Kraig to hell! Blanchard Isle was in the middle of the tropics, the only island that no longer possessed Rock Blood, vegetation, or any living thing except tiny, six-legged sand creepers. Having dried out years ago, it was shelter to the most disgusting group of Horsemen and humans in the world—Flesh Traders. They often stole humans and sometimes even Horsemen, mostly young, orphaned ones, to sell into slavery in the Vertue Mountains.

"When did he leave?" Terra demanded.

Casper shrugged. "Half an hour ago."

Terra glanced skyward then back to Casper.

"Where are you going?" Casper bellowed as Terra galloped toward home.

His first impulse had been to fly after Kraig, but he didn't trust Casper. The man was probably lying. Before he made some foolhardy journey, he'd need to be sure.

Terra's pulse raced with fear when he saw the kicked-in cottage door. The inside was demolished, littered with broken chairs and shards of pottery. A bit of blood had dried on the floor.

"Gods!" He gritted his teeth, raced out of the house, and ascended, circling the meadows, searching for any sign of Inez. Maybe it hadn't been Kraig, but an average thief. In his heart he knew that wasn't the case. Inez would no doubt have successfully defended herself against a human thief, male or female. It was Kraig.

Terra noticed a lone figure running, almost reaching the village. He swooped to a landing in front of Susana. The woman's face was bruised and sweaty, and she gasped for breath.

"Terra, thank the Gods!" Her voice broke. "Kraig took Inez! We tried fighting him, but he was too strong!"

"Did he say where?"

"Something about Blanchard Isle, wherever that is!"

"I know. If he left a short time ago, I'll be able to catch him."

"I'm not exactly sure how long it's been. He knocked me out. They were gone when I came to."

"Can you make it back to the village or are you too badly hurt?"

"I can make it. It's just a few bruises. Hurry, Terra! I'm so afraid of what he'll do to her!"

Terra didn't need any advice about how fast to chase down Kraig. When he caught the bastard, he'd pound the life out of him, as he probably should have done long ago.

* * * * *

"I told you to hurry!" Casper snapped at Kraig.

The Captain and the Horseman faced one another in a small, mossy cave several miles from Hornview. Both clenched their fists and glared at one another.

Inez, groggy from an herbal potion Kraig had forced down her throat when she'd awakened from the whack in the head, lay tied on the packed dirt ground.

"It's been several hours and he's bound to know you didn't take her to Blanchard Isle. He'll be back soon and you need to be out of here!" Casper said.

"I told you, by the time he gets back, he'll be so tired from traveling as well as worrying for her that he won't have a prayer of catching me. I could out-fly him on one of his good days, let alone now. He'll be dropping into the northern seas by midnight and this bitch," Kraig nudged Inez with his Huform foot, "will be frozen to death in the Spikes."

"Even so, I've learned it's best not to take everything for granted," Casper said. "We came this far and we don't want to lose."

"Exactly. Just like we don't want to lose this deal with the Rock Blood traders. As soon as I speak with them, I'll take the woman."

"Why don't I speak with them and you go?"

Kraig uttered a nasty laugh. "Because I don't trust you to make a deal that's in my best interest."

"Just remember, before you leave, announce to the whole village your intentions to drop Inez in the Spikelands, just in case Terra believes it's another lie."

"Yes, and because I know he won't be stupid enough to believe hearsay again, I'll leave him a direct challenge. We'll fight for Inez's life in the Spikelands."

Casper laughed. "As if you'd really fight for her."

"He doesn't know that. He thinks I'd jump at the chance to fight him for any reason, and I can't deny I might have liked a try at him."

"As if you could win."

Kraig's lip curled. "Don't doubt it, *human!*"

"Well, I guess it doesn't matter much. We'll never know."

"That's right. It will be so good to see the mighty Terra and his woman dead in the freezing Spikelands."

* * * * *

Panic over Inez seemed to drive weariness from Terra's mind as well as his body. He flew quickly back to the south, past the villages and directly across the tropical sea toward Blanchard Isle. Scorching heat enveloped him and he tried to keep his heart from pounding out of anger. While fury enforced his strength, it could sap it just as quickly, should it push him past his physical limits. He had several days' worth of rough flights behind him, and his neck still bore bruises from the near strangulation of the previous day. Still, he felt powerful as he soared across islands, green with vegetation, until he saw the barren tan surface of Blanchard Isle.

He landed in the midst of startled Horsemen and grubby, half-naked humans lounging outside the few huts in the center of the island. Panting and sweat-drenched, he glanced around for Inez and Kraig, then headed for the huts.

"What the hell do you want?" demanded a tall Horseman with a coat as tan as the sand beneath his shaggy fetlocks.

"I'm looking for a big reddish Horseman and a black-haired woman he brought in as a slave. She's small with dark skin and dark eyes. Her name is Inez."

"Reddish Horseman?" A nearby human wrinkled his nose. "Ain't got no reddish Horseman working with us, do we Jak?"

The tan Horseman shook his head. "Got no slaves here right now, either. Our next shipment will be in sometime next week. If you're looking to buy yourself a woman, we can—"

"I want *that* woman!" Terra growled, pinning his ears and striding toward the huts.

"What the hell do you think you're doing?" the tan Horseman demanded as Terra began tramping through the huts. The hovels reeked of old sweat and liquor. Other than a few slavers who sprang from their hammocks when he burst inside, the huts were empty. Frustrated, Terra strode back to the island's tiny Running Way.

"We told you!" snapped the Horseman who had greeted him upon landing. "No one's been here in weeks and we're not expecting anyone for another week more!"

"If the Horseman I spoke of brings the woman I described, send a message to me in Hornview. My name is Terra. I'll make it more than worth your while."

The slaver's eyes glowed with greed. "Not a problem. We'll send word if she comes."

Terra nodded, taking a swallow from his half empty water pouch and allowing several moments to catch his breath, though he hated wasting any time. Inez was still trapped with Kraig somewhere, and he had the strangest feeling he'd been sent to the tropics on purpose—not by Susana, who he didn't doubt was a victim herself, but by Kraig. Possibly Casper, too. He needed to get back to Hornview and find out the truth, but not before he replenished his water and questioned people in some of the coastal villages, though he doubted Kraig was in the south. At the speed Terra had traveled, he would have caught up with him.

As he landed in a village to refill his water pouch, Terra took a moment to press his sweaty forehead against the cool rocks on the well and momentarily close his wind-burned eyes.

Terra!

His heart pounded.

Terra! Please, I need you!

Inez! Her voice was as clear to him as it had once been in their shared dreams. They hadn't shared dreams since they'd mated, but there had been stories of the sharing returning after a time.

It's cold, Terra! There are Spikes below!

"Hey, are you all right?" a man nudged Terra's side.

He focused on the short, dark human staring up at him. "You're a Fighting Carrier, aren't you? I didn't think any were due to stop in our village this week."

"I'm passing through," Terra said, corking his water pouch and galloping off. He finally had a clue about where to look for Inez, or so he thought.

* * * * *

By the time Terra landed in Hornview, his every muscle ached from exertion. The almost nonstop flight to and from the tropics then back to the north had begun to take its toll on his already weary body.

He landed on the Running Way, the impact jarring his bones, yet it felt good to be on solid ground again. Pouring sweat, his human chest and equine sides heaving, he needed a few moments to collect himself before taking off for the Spikelands. If only he knew exactly where to go. Perhaps he was insane to even try. Maybe Inez's voice had been a figment of his imagination, brought on by overheating from the tropics. No. He'd never lost his mind before, even under worse conditions.

"Terra!" Susana shouted, racing from the longhouse, a slip of parchment in her hand.

"Terra, I'm so sorry!" she said. "I didn't know he was lying! It seems he planned everything just to hurt you and Inez! He left this!"

Terra opened the parchment with trembling fingers, his heart skipping from his flight as well as from a fresh onslaught of panic. In the message, Kraig claimed to have taken Inez to the fifth island in the Spikelands. He planned to drop her there and wait for Terra. It seemed the bastard wanted a fight. So, Terra had heard Inez's dream voice, after all.

"When did they leave?" Terra gasped.

"Half an hour ago?" Susana shrugged. "Maybe a little less."

Good. Terra had no doubt he could catch Kraig, if he pushed himself hard.

"I have to go." Terra headed for the well to refill his water pouch once more. Then he needed a new Darrion leaf from the tack house. His lungs ached, but thus far he hadn't resorted to mouth breathing. He could make it to the Spikelands. He had to.

Susana followed him, touching a hand to his back and gazing at his wildly heaving flank. Her brow furrowed. "You're overheating."

"I'm fine."

"Terra, are you sure you can make this flight?"

"What choice do I have?"

Susana's brow furrowed and she shook her head. "None. Kraig will kill her, or leave her to die. The Gods only know how many of the islands the Spikes have taken by now."

In the tack house, Terra closed his eyes and trembled, sprouting his full-coat. The denseness of it over his already sweaty skin was uncomfortable at first, but he'd be grateful for it in the Spikelands. He reached for a Darrion leaf while Susana took a bottle of ointment and rubbed it into his legs. He thought briefly of how sensual Inez's hands felt on his legs, but Susana's touch was simply helpful in completing a necessary chore. He wrapped his front legs while Susana bandaged his rear ones.

"You haven't been coughing at all, have you?" asked the healer.

"No."

"Any nose bleeding?"

"None. I said I'll make it."

Susana looked skeptical. "Your sister has already gone for Moor, but I'm going to send a messenger for Linn, too."

Terra glanced at her over his shoulder as he headed back to the Running Way. "Please tell him to hurry."

He hated sounding incompetent, but he wasn't a fool. Everyone had his limits, and he was testing his as they'd never been tested before. He didn't want Inez to suffer for weakness on his part.

As he took off, his wings beating and legs churning, he concentrated solely on Inez. His love for her would give him the heart to bring them both safely home. *His heart.* She was his heart. If he lost her, he lost all.

Terra devoured the skies as he had so many years ago, when he'd set the speed record for Fighting Carriers. Still, he allowed the wind to carry him whenever possible, reserving as much strength as he could for whatever he and Inez would face in the Spikelands. Soon harsh, cold winds whipped around him, stabbing his raw throat and aching chest. A shiver ripped down his spine, spreading icy-cold across his hot legs and belly. A glance below revealed several islands covered with the white frost of the Spikes. Horns of several dead Ice Lizards poked through the whiteness. Sometimes the extreme cold destroyed those powerful beasts as well.

Suddenly he saw a speck in the distance. Ignoring the pain in his lungs, he urged his aching legs and wings faster. Soon he caught sight of Kraig's red hindquarters pumping in the distance. Inez clung to his harness, though he noted Kraig wore no saddle.

Terra edged closer, and Kraig glanced behind him, an expression of shock passing over his full-coated features. So the son-of-a-bitch hadn't really expected him to catch them after all!

Kraig dropped suddenly, and Terra followed. The northernmost island hovered below, already half covered with Spikes. The deadly frost moved rapidly, and soon the entire island would be covered.

Rage enveloped Terra as Kraig landed hard. Had Inez not been such a good rider, she probably would have broken her neck. She tumbled off him, rolling away. As Terra landed, Kraig took off, disappearing in the dark sky.

Terra had no time to chase him. He needed to get Inez off the island before the Spikes killed them both.

"Inez!" Terra shouted as she pushed herself to her feet. She ran to him, slipping on the icy ground.

Without wasting a moment, he picked her up and ascended. Inez's arms clung to his neck and he felt her trembling against him.

He landed on a plateau across the island.

Chapter Nine
Dying For Her

By sheer will alone, Inez kept from crying. She'd been so certain she was going to die without ever holding Terra again. Her head ached from the herbs Kraig had forced her to drink, and as she'd clung to the red Horseman's back, she'd thought she drifted off several times, dreaming of Terra, only to snap awake before falling to her death. Kraig was a choppy flier, not nearly as smooth as Terra or Moor, but what had he cared for her comfort? They hated each other. He was trying to kill her and, she knew, kill Terra as well.

She'd been too groggy to hear Kraig and Casper's entire plan, but it was something about sending Terra south while Kraig killed her in the Spikelands.

Inez clung to Terra in utter relief. He held her close, and she heard him gasping, his full-coat sopping wet and turning cold in the severe Spikeland chill. Shivers ripped through him and his heart slammed beneath her cheek. Steam rose off his hot body against the frigid weather.

Inez tugged away, reaching for his cloak and blanket tucked in the light pleasure saddle he wore. "Here. You'll catch your death."

He pulled the cloak over his man-half while she covered his equine-half with the blanket.

"Gods, you're exhausted." She stared at him.

He couldn't speak for a moment but stood, shaking and gasping. Finally he said, "Give me a little while and we'll go."

"You need more than a little while."

"We don't have it." Terra pointed in the distance. The Spikes were heading for them fast.

"Walk then." She pressed close to him in an attempt to keep her cold human body warm. Just by looking at Terra, she guessed he felt more like dropping than walking, but his common sense won out and he moved slowly across the plateau. He stumbled.

"What's wrong?"

"Just a cramp. It's nothing."

"Where?"

"Left rear leg."

Inez squatted behind him and blew on her cold gloves before rubbing the leg.

"Better?" she called.

"Yes. I have to keep walking, though."

As they walked together, they continued glancing at the fast approaching Spikes. Inez trembled from head to toe. She placed her scarf over her mouth just to breathe without pain.

"We have to go," Terra said, slipping off his cloak and blanket and stuffing them into the saddle pack. "If we stay any longer, I'll be too stiff to fly, and you're already half frozen."

For the first time, Inez felt fear of flying with Terra. She didn't doubt for a second his energy had been spent when he'd landed, and they couldn't have rested for more than half an hour. Still, he was right. The temperature was almost unbearable, and the Spikes were much too close to the plateau.

Terra gave her an arm up. She felt him breathe deeply, collecting himself.

"I'm sorry this happened to you, Inez," he said. "I love you."

"I know." She slipped her arms around his torso and kissed his neck. "I love you, too, Terra. So much."

"I'll get you home. I swear it."

"You'll get us both home, and I'll give you the rubdown of your life."

He glanced at her over his shoulder, his smile just as forced as her own. "You know I live for your rubdowns."

Inez nodded, unable to talk past the lump in her throat. She braced herself as Terra galloped for takeoff. They ascended only moments before the Spikes reached the plateau.

Inez clung to Terra, calling upon all of her skill as a rider to make the journey as easy as possible for him. They seemed lucky at first, as the wind was behind them. Terra was able to coast, giving his tired wings and legs a chance to rest. All too soon, the wind changed, facing them, and he fought to keep on course. A particularly strong gust forced them lower, and she saw the water, the deadly reeds tangled beneath its surface. Terra's muscles bunched as he climbed upward, gasping.

Inez noted he coughed every few moments. Each time she heard the hacking, painful sound and felt his torso jerk, her heart sank. She knew he was suffering, and they still had so long to go.

"What can I do to help you?" Inez called. "Other than jump off your back!"

"Gods," he panted, "don't make me laugh. Not now."

Inez squinted against the frigid winds and buried her face against Terra's hot, pulsing back. She rubbed the joining of his wings, knowing they must hurt as much as his legs and chest.

He seemed to lose power with each passing moment, and Inez wondered how he remained airborne at all. He must have killed himself getting to her, and she vaguely recalled Kraig and Casper saying he'd recently had hard flights in the tropics.

"Terra, I'm unloading the saddle!" she called. He nodded in response, unable to talk while seized by another coughing fit.

Inez reached below, struggling to unfasten the girth. After several moments, she gripped his waist with her knees and dumped the saddle into the water looming all-too-close for her taste.

"The harness?" Terra called, his voice raw as he began loosening one of the straps.

"I don't need it!" Inez told him, her numb fingers loosening the other. It was difficult with the leather soaked from his sweat and cutting into his full-coat. She understood how it must have been uncomfortable. Each forced breath expanded his muscled torso more than usual. Though they'd already loosened it, Inez knew it was long past time they got rid of any unnecessary gear.

With the strap gone, she wrapped her arms around him, loosely, just enough to hold herself steady. With her cheek pressed against his back, she heard each wheezing breath, his respiration much too quick for a Carrier still so far from his destination. His heart slammed against her palms splayed across his chest, and she wondered which would explode first, his lungs or his heart, sending them both to their death amidst the flesh-eating plants below. Maybe his legs or wings would fail. She knew the cramps in his rear leg had returned several times during the journey. He'd managed to work them out while in the sky, but by now every muscle in his body must be on fire.

"I love you, Terra," she shouted, knowing his only chance to survive would be to fly for himself. "I'm getting off!"

"Inez!" he snarled, his voice raw. "You die and I die!"

She paused, her eyes fixed on the sea below. Survival instinct battled with her love for him.

"Inez!" he gasped, shuddering as another coughing fit racked his body. "I'll follow you. I swear—"

"Quiet!" she screamed, knowing he meant every word. "I'm not going anywhere!"

They pushed forward. Inez felt as helpless as when she'd watched her family die from the Plague. She couldn't help them, and she couldn't help Terra. Or could she?

"I love you, Terra!" she called above the wind. "I know you can fly this! Kraig thought he'd beat you, but he's a fool! You're more of a Carrier than he'll ever be, and you're proving it!"

* * * * *

Terra never imagined it possible to fly through such pain. Every muscle in his body felt as if it had been chewed and spat out by an Ice Lizard. His nose, throat and chest were on fire. No matter how he tried repressing the cough, it burst past his lips, sending swords through his lungs along with the flames. He tasted blood and couldn't tell if it resulted from the cough or the streams running from his nose. Of all the hundreds of flights he'd taken, he'd never bled. Somewhere in the back of his exhausted mind, he felt saddened. He hoped he hadn't done himself permanent damage, yet if he had, it would be worth it, providing he brought Inez to safety. She was all that mattered now. He wondered if she realized how much her words of love sustained him. Knowing she believed in him forced him toward home. He'd reached his limits long ago, but managed to keep flying. He had to. He was a Fighting Carrier, made to endure when other Horsemen surrendered. Now, all his training, all his strength, were focused on one important task—saving this woman whom he loved as much as his own life.

The wind finally lessened and warmed. Thank the Gods they were out of the Spikelands!

Terra sank lower, his vision blurred from pain and exhaustion. His entire body was aflame now and he shook so hard he wondered how Inez managed to stay on his back.

"We're almost there!" Inez shouted, her gentle palms rubbing his sore chest as she had throughout the hellish flight. "I knew you could do it, Terra! There's the coast. Just a little more and we'll be home!"

Terra took her word for it. His eyes were far too blurry to discern much. He dipped lower and finally saw the shoreline. Gods, he wanted to drop right onto the beach, but he knew he was injured badly. He needed help, and the only way to get it was to land on the Running Way.

* * * * *

Casper sat in the longhouse, feeling happier than he ever remembered. He and Kraig had made so many extra coins selling the stolen Rock Blood that soon he could leave Hornview and settle somewhere without a stinking Horseman in sight.

Though Kraig had arrived home angry because Terra had actually caught up to him before he dumped Inez in the Spikelands, the redhead assured him the couple wouldn't make it home.

"I saw him," Kraig had sneered. "He caught me, all right, but he was half dead doing it."

"He caught you directly after making a flight to the tropics and back. Makes you wonder about your own endurance, doesn't it, Kraig?" Casper had grinned, his eyes sweeping the redhead's drenched body and trembling legs as he'd walked himself out after his nonstop flight to the Spikelands and back.

Though Casper didn't care a thing for Horsemen, he'd heard talk in the village that Kraig might be strong enough and fast enough to break Terra's speed record. Fast enough was one thing, but strong enough? Casper doubted it. Kraig was powerful before reaching his limit, but both of them had witnessed Terra's sustained strength. When he'd landed that night after carrying two men and cargo, his legs had stood strong.

"Don't bother me!" Kraig's strength seemed to flood back in the face of his anger. His pointed ears pressed close to his head as he used his equine body to push Casper backwards.

"I don't care which Horseman is faster." Casper shrugged. "And neither should you. He's dead now, remember?"

Dead! Casper grinned as he finished his meal. He stared at Susana across the table. The little healer looked worried, and he knew she had reason. Her Horseman lover had just arrived and, with the older Horseman, Moor, was preparing to search for Terra.

Susana stood and walked outside. Casper followed for curiosity's sake. He wanted to enjoy the frenzy of the Horsemen, Susana and the beast-bitch Phillipa.

Leaning against the side of the tack house, he watched as the entire pitiful group emerged.

"Please be careful," Susana said.

"We will," Linn assured her.

Before they could speak further, the sound of wings beating overhead drew their attention.

"Damn!" Casper breathed. *Terra!*

"Gods, it's them!" Phillipa shouted.

"Look at his flight pattern! He's in distress!" Linn bellowed, he and Moor galloping toward the Running Way, Phillipa racing after them.

"I need to get my supply bag!" Susana said, rushing into the longhouse.

Cursing under his breath, Casper hurried off to inform Kraig of their failure.

* * * * *

Inez's heart pounded in fear, both for Terra's life and her own, as he dropped rapidly toward the Running Way. She knew because of his fast-slipping control, the landing would be hard.

She braced herself, grunting as he struck the ground and crashed to his knees. Inez flew off his back, gasping as the wind whooshed from her body on impact with the ground. She pushed herself onto her hands and knees and scrambled toward Terra who lay on his side, shaking and coughing.

"No," Inez murmured, using the back of her hand to wipe blood from his nose and lips. *Gods no!* she thought, no longer speaking her fears aloud.

Strong arms embraced her from behind. She glanced up at Moor, grateful to see him.

Linn arrived next, kneeling beside Terra and placing a hand on his lathered body. "He's burning up. Moor, help me get the trough."

The two Horsemen galloped off just as Phillipa raced onto the Running Way.

"I'll get water!" Phillipa shouted, running toward the well.

Several villagers, having noticed the commotion, rushed over. Susana pushed her way through them and knelt by Terra, taking his face in her hands and beginning her examination.

"Tell them to heat water at the longhouse!" she ordered the villagers, and they took off. The healer glanced at Inez. "He needs warmth on his chest."

Phillipa arrived with a bucket, and Susanna shouted, "Wait, don't throw that water! Give me some for this mixture."

Susana opened her bag and pulled out a mug which she dipped into the bucket. She stirred in powdered herbs and motioned for Phillipa to empty the rest of the water on Terra's overheated body. She doused his hindquarters and ran for another bucket.

"Inez, help him get this down." Susana held out the mug.

Inez sat on her knees and lifted Terra's heavy torso against her chest. He was coughing so much it was nearly impossible for the two women to force the medicine down his throat.

"We have water!" Linn said. He and Moor stood, a trough from the village's central barn held between them.

Susana and Inez managed to help Terra drink the last of the herbs. The healer stepped aside but Inez refused to drop Terra on the Running Way while Linn and Moor emptied the contents of the trough over his entire body.

"Get another one," Susana told them.

"What do you want me to do?" Inez asked. If she actively helped, she'd keep from giving in to tears.

"Just stay with him," Susana told her. "After we cool him off more, Linn and Moor can help him back to the longhouse and we'll put warm compresses on his chest."

By the time Phillipa, Moor and Linn arrived with more water, Susana's herbs had taken effect and Terra's coughing lessened. Though he still panted hard, his wheezing had stopped, and the water seemed to have cooled his body to a less dangerous temperature.

"Inez?" he whispered in a raw voice.

"I'm here." She kissed the damp black hair on his forehead as his eyes slipped shut.

Linn stooped beside them and used his arms to support Terra, giving Inez's much smaller frame some relief. The youth shook him gently. "Terra! We need to get you to the longhouse."

Terra moaned, and Inez wasn't sure if he'd fully comprehended Linn's words.

"That was a terrible landing, Sir!" Linn said. Terra's eyes opened slowly and focused on Linn who offered him a teasing smile. "Not by the book at all!"

"Damn insolent recruit," Terra murmured, pushing himself upward with Linn's help. His legs nearly collapsed under him, but Moor caught his hindquarters and held him steady.

Phillipa had hitched Black Silk and another true-horse from the village to a rig and drove it onto the Running Way. With Linn and Moor's help, Terra got onto the rig with Inez and Susana and rode back to the village. By then, he was able to walk into the longhouse where he dropped onto blankets the villagers had arranged by the fire.

Inez and Susana brought a bucket of hot water beside him and soaked towels, placing one across Terra's chest and switching it with another when it cooled. He drifted off while Inez removed the bandages from his legs and massaged his body.

Moor—now in Huform—approached and said, "You'd better change your wet clothes, Inez, before you get sick, too."

"Come," Susana said, "I have a tunic you can borrow."

Inez, hesitant to leave Terra, followed Susana to her small room in a corner of the longhouse and removed her clothes.

"Will he be all right?" Inez asked as Susana handed her a tunic.

"He's alive," Susana said.

"But will he be able to fly again?"

"Fly. Yes. Fast and far, I don't know."

"Living without speed will be worse than death for him," Inez murmured, tears threatening to spill. "And it's because of me."

"No." Susana squeezed Inez's shoulder. "It's because of Kraig. His hatred and jealousy did this. Terra loves you so much, Inez. He did the impossible for you. He shouldn't have been able to make this last flight, but he did, and I promise I will do everything I can to see that he heals."

Inez nodded. "I know you will. Thank you, Susana."

"With plenty of rest, there's a good chance for him to recover completely. He's very strong."

"Yes, he is. It's almost frightening, having someone love me this much."

"I can see how it would be. But it's also rare. You're lucky."

"Probably luckier than I deserve."

"No. Because I believe you love him just as much."

Inez and Susana returned to Terra. Inez paused, drawing a sharp breath as he shuddered so hard ripples reached her through the wooden floor. Her eyes widened when the wings and legs of his equine-half seemed to mold into his body, creating a single, talon-like tail covered in short, dark hair.

So this is what shapeshifting looks like, Inez thought. Terra was right. It wasn't attractive, but she didn't care. She loved him too much and knew how beautiful the final result was.

Terra moaned. Moor placed a firm hand on his shoulder. "Just a little more. It's almost done."

Terra shuddered again and his full-coat disappeared. Only the long, curly black human hair remained on his head, leaving his man-half as well as the talon covered in bare flesh. Then the talon seemed to mold before her eyes to the pair of long, muscular human legs, pelvis, testicles and cock so familiar to Inez.

She knelt beside him, covering him with a blanket. His eyes opened and fixed on her.

"You saw?" he murmured.

"I saw."

His brow furrowed. "And?"

"And you're right. It's ugly." She smiled, kissing his mouth. "I love you so much, Terra."

"I love you, too, Inez."

Moor and Susana left them alone by the fire. Inez lay down beside him, stroking his face, feeling the comforting heat of his body, and thankful they both had survived.

Chapter Ten
By the Fire

Casper, his heart thumping, stepped silently into the longhouse. Hours ago, when he'd informed Kraig that Terra and Inez still lived, the redheaded Horseman had thrown such a fit of rage that Casper feared for his own life. Kraig's enormous hooves had beaten the walls of the cave where he hid their stolen supplies of Rock Blood, sending chunks of stone flying and threatening to collapse the mossy hovel.

"Now what are we going to do about it?" Casper snapped, once Kraig stood, panting, his teeth and fists clenched.

"We? I've done my part, nearly killing myself on a nonstop trip back and forth to the Spikelands! The rest of the village knows my part in the bitch Inez's abduction, so I certainly can't burst into the village and finish the job! It's up to you."

"Absolutely not!" Casper laughed humorlessly.

"Why? We're both just about ready to leave this village and settle somewhere else with the wealth we've earned from pilfering the Rock Blood. You said yourself the longhouse is just about empty at night, with the Chieftain and his servants in the sleeping quarters. Even if they're not, how many servants would speak against the Captain of the Guard?"

"Probably more than you think, if it came to harming Terra and Inez. They're well-liked by the common folk of Hornview. Far more than I."

"Then don't be seen! If you refuse to hold up your end of this bargain, I'll make sure everyone in the village knows your part in our crimes."

"You'll be captured yourself."

"By whom? You said yourself Linn has already returned to the Hall of Fighting Carriers, and Moor is too slow to catch me. Terra will probably never fly again, from what you've told me. I'll tell all and fly away. Think about it before you turn coward in our schemes, human!"

Seething, Casper made his way across the longhouse. He should have known better than to make plans with a stinking Horseman!

A quick glance around the longhouse revealed it was empty, except for a servant boy sleeping in a far corner of the room and Terra, half-dazed in yet another fit of coughing, by the fire.

Casper smiled wickedly as he approached. With his pasty face streaked with bloody spittle he was too weak to wipe away, the mighty Fighting Carrier looked like trash.

Glancing around again, surprised the Horseman's loving wife and attentive nurses had left him alone in such a vulnerable position, Casper assured himself he was safe to continue his task. Still, he knew enough to hurry. He'd already loaded his belongings into Kraig's cave, and the redheaded Horseman hid outside, having grudgingly agreed to fly Casper to his escape once he'd murdered Terra. Inez no longer mattered much to Casper. He knew it would be far worse for her to live while Terra died.

Casper stood over Terra, his hand tight on his sword. He couldn't resist watching his enemy writhe, his broad shoulders and back, once so powerful, now hunched in agony as he coughed up his life. Casper pulled back his foot and kicked Terra hard in his lower back before raising his sword.

Searing pain shot through Casper's back and chest, spreading to his fingertips as he dropped the sword before it struck home.

Gasping, his eyes wide, he tried yanking away whatever weapon had rammed between his shoulder blades. Inez, her eyes fierce with rage, shoved him hard.

* * * * *

Inez stared at Casper who lay on his back, the point of a dagger protruding through his chest, blood bubbling from his mouth. His eyes stared wide with shock, even in death.

Trembling from rage and disgust at what she'd been forced to do, Inez hurried to Terra's side. She helped him to a more comfortable sitting position and wiped his face before applying another warm cloth to his chest. His eyes were unfocused and pain-hazed, and she doubted he'd even been aware of how close he'd come to death—again. She was almost glad he was still so out of it, since that vicious kick in his Turning Point would have been excruciating otherwise.

She'd left him for a few short moments to ask Susana for more herbs to ease his cough. When she came back, she found Casper kicking her husband, a sword poised to kill in his hands. She'd gone mad with fury. Instinctively, she'd reached for a dagger resting by a bowl of fruit on the table and attacked Casper. Now she thought she might be sick. Not that he didn't deserve to die, but she'd never killed anyone in her life.

"Gods, what happened?" Susana gasped, placing the mug of herbs on the table and kneeling beside Casper.

"He tried to kill Terra," Inez said.

Susana shook her head, bringing the mug to Inez. "Make him drink this. I'll get Moor and the Chieftain."

As the healer hurried off, Inez managed to help Terra empty the contents of the mug. Within moments, the potion took effect and he rested quietly.

"Inez," he murmured.

"Yes?" She changed the cooling cloth for a warmer one and covered him with the blanket he'd thrown off while coughing.

"What happened? Casper..."

"Don't worry about it," she soothed as he drifted back to sleep.

Sitting beside him, she sighed, running a hand through her hair. What had she said about it being a wonderful winter?

* * * * *

Less than a week later, due to his powerful shapeshifter constitution, Terra's cough improved and his severe chest pain faded. Inez knew they could have moved back to their cottage, but at Moor and Susana's advice, decided to remain at the longhouse until Terra regained more strength.

"That bastard Kraig is still out there," Moor had warned. "We've had search parties but haven't located him. Still, we've found all the evidence we need to prove he and Casper were behind the Rock Blood theft in our village and several neighboring ones. He's a disgrace to Carriers, and I don't trust him not to try killing you again, Terra, and Inez along with you just for the fun of it. Moving out to that cottage by yourselves at this time would be suicide."

"And don't be getting that mean look on your face." Phillipa had pointed a finger at her brother. "Use common sense — at least for Inez's sake. I can understand you nearly killing yourself on that last flight. You didn't have a choice and any husband worth his skin would have done the same, but now there's no reason for anyone to be in danger."

"You're still a brat with a big mouth." Terra curled his lip at Phillipa.

"But I'm right. And you're still an arrogant son-of-a-mule!"

"Nice way to talk about Father."

"You know I was insulting you and not Father! Speaking of Father, you're just like him! His own arrogance got him killed on a flight he shouldn't have been on in the first place. If you want to die like a fool too, go ahead!" Phillipa bellowed and stalked out of the longhouse, but not before Inez noticed tears in her eyes.

Inez stood. "I'm going to talk to her."

She tracked Phillipa to the stable where she was brushing Black Silk's coat with a vengeance.

"He's going to stay at the longhouse," Inez said. "If I have to tie him there."

Phillipa wiped her eyes on her shoulder. "He's such a donkey's ass."

"Yes, but I like him that way." Inez grinned, taking another brush and helping Phillipa groom the stallion. "Even if he is harder to care for than a true-horse."

The women glanced at each other and chuckled.

Moments later, Terra stepped inside. "Is this a private party or can I join?"

"Private party," Phillipa said. "Women only."

"Then why does he get to stay?" Terra grinned, patting Black Silk's rump.

"Because he has *horse sense*." Inez stared hard into her husband's eyes.

Terra groaned. "That was horrible, woman, but I understand. We'll stay in the village for a while longer, if you want."

Inez had noted the tenseness in Terra's jaw and the fury in his eyes as he agreed. Admitting any weakness was an affront to his very nature, particularly when that weakness included the inability to protect his wife.

Inez stopped brushing Phillipa's stallion and wrapped her arms around the neck of her own. "It *is* what I want."

Terra kissed her and winked. "But any longer than a week and we'll need privacy."

Inez blushed and stole a glance at Phillipa who guided Black Silk back to his stall. "Glad to see at least someone can control you, Terra."

"I'm about as controllable as you are."

Phillipa shrugged. "Runs in the family."

As the tall, black-haired woman walked past them, Terra gripped her shoulder. "Thanks for all you've done, Phillipa."

Phillipa smiled and placed her hand over Terra's before leaving the couple alone.

"She's like Rock Blood." Terra sighed. "Hard on the outside, liquid on the inside. I guess that's how many women are."

"Not me," Inez murmured.

"You are, too, except I've seen your liquid turn hot enough to boil."

"As Casper found out." Inez lowered her eyes. "Do you think less of me now that I've killed a man?"

He laughed. "Less of you? You saved my life."

"I owed you."

"You owe me nothing. I'd fly to my death for you without hesitation. And don't think Kraig will go unpunished for what he's done."

"Terra—"

"No man hurts my wife and flies off to live happily on stolen wealth."

"If he's gone, Terra, can't you just leave it at that?"

"And spend the rest of our lives wondering if he'll creep back to finish what he started? I won't live like that, Inez."

She sighed, resting her cheek against his chest. It didn't surprise her that he wanted revenge. In truth, she wouldn't sleep another peaceful night knowing Kraig was still out there, perhaps plotting against Terra again.

"Just heal first," she said.

He stroked her hair and kissed the top of her head. "I will. I feel much better already."

Neither of them mentioned that it was unknown whether or not he still had the ability to fly fast or long. She knew he refused to believe he couldn't, and until they found out for sure, she wouldn't sour his dreams with her concerns. One thing she did know, if he had been permanently damaged, then he hadn't a prayer of avenging them against Kraig.

* * * * *

It was another two weeks before Terra and Inez moved back to their cottage, and another week more before Terra attempting flying. Susana said she would have preferred he wait longer, but Terra refused.

"I feel fine. The cough is gone, and I'm going insane from lack of exercise," he said on the morning of his test flight as he stood in the field behind the cottage, Inez and Susana beside him.

"You've been cantering every day," Inez said. "What more do you want? You almost died, Terra!"

"I remember."

"Just be careful," Susana said. "If you feel any pain or start coughing, I want you down immediately. And no carrying anything or anybody for at least another week."

"Yes, ma'am." Terra saluted the healer.

Inez slapped his rock-hard shoulder. "This isn't a joking matter!"

"Believe me, ladies, I have no desire to be lying like a corpse again, unable to defend what's mine. Now, if you'll excuse me, I need to gallop for takeoff."

Inez drew a deep breath, her entire body tense as Terra began at a walk, his pace increasing until his legs seemed to blur as they swallowed the snowy field.

Suddenly his magnificent black wings spread, beating as he ascended.

Terra formed a wide circle overhead, rising higher until he was a black speck in the clear winter sky. He circled three more times before swooping lower. Only when his hooves touched the ground in a graceful, perfect landing did Inez relax. She and Susana jogged toward him as he cantered in their direction, a brilliant smile on his face.

He reached out and tugged Inez close. His breathing was scarcely quicker than normal and she sensed his heart pounded against her cheek more from excitement than exertion. His chest rumbled with laughter and his ears twitched. "That felt so damn good!"

Susana grinned. "That was a little higher and faster than I would have liked to see, but I'm guessing you feel fine?"

"I feel fantastic!" Terra held Inez at arm's length and kissed her firmly on the mouth before gazing skyward. "I'm going again."

"Remember, don't wear yourself out," Susana warned. "I want you to gradually work to your maximum, and any sign at all of the cough returning, stop."

"I will." Terra's blue eyes glistened. "But it won't come back. I feel it."

Inez stood on tiptoe and kissed him again, pride filling her heart. It felt wonderful to see Terra healthy and happy again. She had no doubt that within a few months, he'd be back in top condition. His goal was to be fully prepared for Gathering season. Even if he wasn't quite ready, it wouldn't matter. The idea that he could fly and run again meant the most. She could convince him to wait until the next year's season, if she had to.

As Terra ascended again, Susana glanced at Inez. "Looks like I'm not needed here."

"You think he'll be all right?"

"Inez, as high and fast as he soared the first time, if his lungs were going to give him trouble, he'd have felt it then. Just make sure he doesn't get too overheated and overworked. All he needs to use is common sense and he'll be busting himself again on Gatherings sooner than you realize."

"He better never bust himself again like on that last trip."

"I hope not," Susana agreed. "I have to get back to the village. I'm cooking supper for Linn tonight."

"Bye. Thanks again for coming out."

"My patient's first flight after recovery. I wouldn't miss it." Susana winked.

As her friend started walking back to the village, Inez turned her attention to Terra as he soared overhead. She sighed. It felt so good for things to be returning to normal again.

Close to an hour later, after gradually slowing his flight, Terra landed. Inez noted he wasn't perspiring heavily and his breathing was good. The delight hadn't faded from his eyes, but appeared to have increased.

"My form was a little off," he said as they walked together so he could completely cool down before returning to the cottage.

"Not at all."

"Maybe you couldn't see it, but I could feel it. I have to work on that—after I work on you, that is." Terra nuzzled her neck.

"I'm looking forward to it." She giggled as his tongue tickled her ear. Though he'd been in the mood for lovemaking only a few weeks after his illness, it was only recently that his incredible stamina had returned and provided her with carnal sessions morning, noon and night.

It didn't take long for Terra to cool, and afterward Inez gave him a rubdown that had them both more than ready for lovemaking. She watched as he shifted shape outside the cottage. Now that his health had returned, the shifting itself wasn't the slow process she'd seen that night in the longhouse. With a simple closing of his eyes and a single shudder that sent ripples through the ground beneath him, he molded from four legs to two so fast the talon-like tail was hardly visible.

"I'm so glad you'll change in front of me now." Inez buried her face in his chest as he tugged her against the length of his naked Huform. She felt him shiver in the snowy winter wind. "I feel like there's finally no secrets between us."

"You've seen me at my most unattractive." Terra kissed her brow. "I guess before I was afraid if you found the change too ugly, you wouldn't want to be with me, and I couldn't stand the thought of losing you."

"You'll never lose me, Terra. I love you more than anything or anybody. How could I ever deny the man who shares my dreams?"

He held her gaze for a long moment. They knew they were luckier than many human/Horseman couples, since their shared dreams had returned after mating. Not often, but every now and then, they would awaken, wrapped in each other's arms and smile, knowing the visions behind their closed eyes had been an emotional joining. It was the same kind of joining that had brought them together — the same that bound them during those moments when Inez had clung, semi-conscious, to Kraig while Terra had succumbed to a moment of exhaustion, closing his eyes at the well in the southern village.

Terra covered her lips with his, his tongue stroking her teeth, lips and the soft, moist skin inside her cheeks.

"Let's get inside before you freeze to death." She slapped his muscular buttocks.

Hand in hand, they jogged to the bathhouse. He jumped in the hot spring water while she ripped off her clothes and joined him.

"This bathhouse is the best investment we ever made!" Terra grinned as he swam to her and held her close, nibbling her ear.

"Definitely! It was coin well spent." She slipped her legs around his waist as he pressed her to the edge of the spring and devoured her lips, his tongue searching her mouth.

After washing each other's hair and bodies with a cake of lavender-scented soap, Terra hoisted himself to the edge of the pool and retrieved towels and robes from a trunk in the corner. He dried off briskly, watching as Inez stepped out of the pool. Immediately, he draped her in one of the towels and rubbed her from shoulder to ankle. While she wrapped the towel around her hair, he held open a robe for her. She slipped into it, fastening the belt as she watched him shrug on his.

"I'll beat you to the cottage!" She sprinted out of the bathhouse, laughing at her own stupidity when he passed her so fast he'd already reached the cottage and torn off his robe before she arrived at the door.

"So much for beating a Horseman no matter what form he's in." She wrinkled her nose, closing the door behind her.

"Guess what? I'll share my prize for winning." Terra tugged her in front of the hearth and undressed her, tossing her robe onto a chair. When she was naked, he drew her into his arms and kissed her forehead, nose and lips.

His tongue swept from one nipple to the other until she sighed, wiggling her hips as pleasure grew. Sinking to his knees in front of her, he kissed her belly and her pelvis. Inez moaned when his hands gripped her buttocks and his tongue flicked her clit. He used his lips to tug the soft nubbin while one of his hands moved to her pussy. His finger circled the damp lips before pushing inside her.

Inez buried her fingers in his hair as he swirled his tongue inside her. When she came, her legs nearly buckled. Terra caught her, guiding her onto the rug in front of the hearth. He sat, his legs stretched out in front of him, and tugged her close. With his hard cock snug in her hot, wet pussy and her legs stretched on either side of his waist, they clung to each other, rocking and stroking. Inez's eyes fixed on his intense blue gaze. Moaning softly as passion grew, she forced her eyes to remain open, wanting to watch him.

"Oh Terra!" she cried, her fingers biting into his rounded biceps.

"Talk to me, woman!"

"I love you! I love you so much!" she gasped, teetering on the verge of orgasm.

His eyes blurred with passion and his lashes fluttered before closing completely. His lips parted as his breathing grew ragged. His head arched back, the veins and tendons standing out in his thick neck, flushed from desire. That lusty pink tinge spread across his high cheekbones and darkened the flesh of his muscled chest, visible beneath a dusting of black hair.

Watching his arousal drove Inez to the breaking point. Her eyes closed against her will and she climaxed, quaking from head to toe with breath-stealing waves of pleasure.

"Oh Gods, Inez!" he gasped. She felt him straining for control of his desire. When the last ripple coursed through her, he moved her onto her back. Instinctively, Inez's legs wrapped around his waist as he thrust, his weight supported on his hands.

Her eyes remained tightly closed as her desire rekindled.

"Terra, oh, Terra!" she chanted. "Please don't stop! Please!"

He lowered himself enough to kiss her, his tongue rimming her lips before it plunged into her mouth in time with his thrusting hips. Inez's hips lifted to meet his, her legs squeezing his waist as she clung to his neck. Waves of climax broke over her and she cried out, clinging to him even tighter. Beneath his brisk rhythm, another orgasm built almost before the last one ended.

"Inez! Hell and damnation, woman!" he growled, his voice raw with lust, his body hot and damp as he pushed her to one last climax that carried him with it. He rammed hard, his body throbbing against hers as he collapsed on top of her.

"Ohh." Inez grinned, feeling their slowing heartbeats and breathing return to normal. "I think this *is* turning out to be a wonderful winter after all."

Chapter Eleven
Sky Fight
The Tropics
10 Months Later

Inez wiped her sweaty face with the damp sleeve of her thin cotton shirt before replacing her hat and helping Terra load his saddle packs with Rock Blood. Around them, other Carriers and Gatherers loaded their packs and prepared for the flight back to the village.

Terra had been asked to fill in again for another injured Horseman, and this time, with the danger of the Plague having passed, he'd gladly agreed to Inez riding him. Besides, since Kraig had never been found, he was reluctant to leave her alone, and Inez admitted she loved his constant company.

Since recovering from last year's near-fatal flight, Terra was fitter than ever, surpassing even his old praiseworthy endurance. Inez felt proud to have been with him every step of the way, feeling the power in his magnificent Horseman body as he galloped over fields and soared across the sky.

"This hasn't been a bad a trip at all," Terra said. "Didn't even get attacked."

"The tropical lizards don't seem as eager for fights as the ones in the north."

"In the tropical climate, they have a bigger natural supply of food. They don't always see supper every time a party flies in." Terra affectionately stroked Inez's upper arms with his fingertips.

With the last of the saddle packs fastened securely, Inez withdrew a wooden container filled with a thick, herbal paste that reminded her of clear ooze. It smelled nice, though, and protected both her and Terra from the strong tropical sun.

"Let me." He slipped off her shirt, revealing her curvaceous body covered only by a thin strip of cloth across her breasts, molded with sweat to her skin. Draping her shirt over his shoulder, he dipped his fingers into the container she held, rubbed his hands together, and massaged it over her shoulders, arms, and back while she lathered her breasts and belly. Leaning close, he whispered in her ear, "I wish I could do your front, too, but we'd cause a scandal."

She grinned, playfully slapping the side of his head before offering him more from the jar. He spread the paste over his damp chest, arms, and belly. Inez stood on a rock and mounted him. He held the container up to her and she loaded her hands with the paste, spreading it over his slick shoulders and back with slow, sensual strokes as she whispered, "I wish I could have done your front, too."

After ensuring all the riders and Carriers were ready, Terra ordered the takeoff and they departed.

Inez had to agree with Terra that, except for less lizard attacks, the southern flights were as difficult as the northern ones. She knew he and most of the other Carriers particularly hated the tropics due to the heat.

She noted that after landings his strength was often visibly drained and he took forever to cool down. The smaller Carriers fared better in the tropics, whereas the bigger ones seemed built for the harsh winds and frigid cold in the north.

"Well, after tomorrow, we'll be on our way home," Terra panted as, hours later, his hooves struck the Running Way in another perfect landing. Had her eyes been closed, Inez wouldn't have even known when they left the air.

"I can hardly wait," Inez said, tugging at the clinging front of her wet shirt before dismounting and helping Terra unpack.

"I can hardly wait to cool down."

Inez didn't blame him. She felt uncomfortably hot and sticky, so she could only imagine how he, with his hot Horseman's physique, felt. Sweat poured from him in rivulets. Even the end of his braid dripped down the gleaming flesh of his man-half. His horse-body was streaming, so she knew he couldn't wait to tear off the saddle and drenched blanket beneath.

"Let's head right to the river after we unpack," she suggested.

"Sounds great to me." He flashed her a grin. "And how about spending some time in the secluded little cove after I shift to Huform?"

"Ohh," she shivered with desire at his carnal implication, "let's hurry."

Once the packs were loaded into one of the villager's carts and brought to a storage house, Inez held Terra's harness while he removed the saddle and blanket. They dropped everything in the tack house and headed for the river.

"Hello!" A dark, lanky villager waved to Terra. "I was hoping to catch you."

"What is it?"

"A Horseman called Linn landed while you were at the Gathering. He's waiting in the men's bathhouse and asked me to get you when you landed."

"Was something wrong?"

"I don't think so. He said he thought you'd want to know he's been stationed here for a while."

Terra and Inez exchanged an odd look. Linn was now a permanent trainer at the Hall of Fighting Carriers. With his new recruits about to take their final test, it was strange for him to be shipped out to join southern Gatherings.

"I'm going to find out what happened. I'll tell him to join us at the lake. Be right back, my love." Terra kissed her cheek before heading for the men's bathhouse across the village.

No sooner had he disappeared than Inez felt a hand clamp over her mouth and an arm wrap around her waist, crushing her ribs.

"Good afternoon, sweetheart!" a familiar voice rasped close to her ear. *Kraig!*

She tried to scream and struggle, but he ascended fast. Inez's heart pounded in sheer terror as the Horseman burst through the cover of tropical trees, his red wings beating hard as he climbed higher and higher.

* * * * *

Terra glanced around the bathhouse as human males and Horsemen in Huform cast him odd looks.

"Excuse me," Terra said, knowing most shapeshifters never entered public bathhouses sporting their equine-half. "I'm looking for a friend. Name's Linn."

The men exchanged glances and shook their heads. Terra's brow furrowed, an odd feeling settling in his chest, before shouts erupted from outside. He turned fast, nearly knocking over a Gatherer, and cantered to the village square. A group of villagers pointed skyward where a reddish blur was fast ascending.

"He took Inez!" a Gatherer bellowed to Terra. "That Horseman took her and flew off!"

Terra knew who had taken her, and this time Kraig would pay with his life!

His pulse racing with rage and fear of Inez being hurt, Terra ascended faster than he ever imagined possible. Later, humans and Horsemen alike told stories of the ascent in wonder, saying the Fighting Carrier looked like a streak of black lightning flashing in the wrong direction.

Terra soared, his gaze fixed on Kraig and Inez who had reached a height dangerous to human and Horseman. Terra began to feel lightheaded from the elevation, yet within moments he caught up to them.

Kraig forced a grin, his chest heaving, Inez, unconscious from the altitude, hanging precariously in his arms.

"Happy landing!" Kraig panted, dropping Inez.

If a man could die of fear, Terra knew he would have at that moment. Instead he flipped over and dropped so fast the rush of wind stole his breath and blurred his eyes. Still, he could see Inez falling below. Beating his wings, he reached her, pulling her close to his chest, his heart slamming so hard he thought he might black out.

"Oh Gods, woman," he murmured, kissing her forehead as she opened groggy eyes.

"Damn," Inez groaned. "It's him again, Terra."

"Not for long," Terra snarled through gritted teeth as he tilted his face upward at Kraig who flew west, nearly out of sight.

When Terra landed, several villagers took Inez and guided her to a bench.

"Are you all right?" Terra stared into her eyes.

She nodded.

"I'm going to kill him," Terra snarled.

Whether or not she protested, he didn't know and didn't care. He ascended again, his wings and legs racing on the wind, as he pursued Kraig.

Within moments he flew so close to Kraig that he could see the sweat flying from the redhead's heated body and the green of his eyes when he glared at Terra over his shoulder, his ears pressed flat to the sides of his head.

Terra was at his heels when Kraig kicked backwards with his rear legs, knocking Terra in his equine-chest just below his man-belly.

Terra spun, lunging hard, his front legs landing on Kraig's back.

The redhead dropped fast as he struggled beneath Terra's weight. He reached behind and grasped a handful of Terra's hair, yanking it out at the roots. One of Terra's fists smashed Kraig between his equine shoulders. He grunted, flipping over and flying on his back in an attempt to unload Terra, but he held fast.

Terra was determined Kraig would not fly away free again. The only way he was descending today was as a dead Horseman.

Kraig rolled again, fast, and Terra slipped. The two Horsemen were suddenly locked, face-to-face, in a tangle of stomping equine legs and jabbing human fists.

"I'm going to kill you and then your woman!" Kraig roared, his fist slamming Terra's mouth. Blood flew on the wind.

"When donkeys fly!" Terra bellowed. One of Terra's palms struck Kraig hard in the throat, cutting off his wind, while one of his hooves rammed him in the belly. Kraig grasped his throat, his eyes wide and wings faltering. Terra spun, his back hooves smashing across Kraig's face, knocking him unconscious. Time seemed to freeze as the redhead dropped fast. The eerie stillness was broken by the sickening impact of his body smashing on the rocks poking above the rushing river water. Terra's heart slammed in his chest as he stared at Kraig's twisted, bloody corpse. For the past several months, he and Moor had used all their spare time to search for Kraig, longing for revenge and fearful that he might one day return to do further harm. Today Terra's worst nightmare had almost come true. He'd nearly lost Inez to Kraig's evil.

Inez!

He turned quickly, ready to fly back to the village, but he heard two voices shouting for him from below. Inez, astride another Carrier from the village, waved to him.

Terra descended, flying alongside the other Carrier as they landed. With a quick thank you to her host, Inez jumped off his back and into Terra's waiting arms.

"I love you!" She clung to him, covering his hot, heaving chest with kisses. He bent and captured her lips, his palms caressing her shoulders and back.

"Gods, Inez, I've never been so afraid in my life as when I saw him drop you." Terra held her close, closing his eyes. "I love you so much."

"It's over. He's dead."

Terra nodded, his face buried in her shoulder.

The other Carrier, a slender roan, approached with a nervous grin. "Were you trying to set a new speed record or something? I've never seen a Horseman go that fast."

"It's called fear." Terra winked.

"No," Inez squeezed him hard, "it's Terra."

* * * * *

Inez rubbed Terra's shoulders as her legs hugged his equine sides. He plodded down the road to their cottage, glad they were finally out of the tropics.

"I can't wait to see Moor and Susana," Inez said. "At least now none of us have to worry about Kraig anymore."

"You know," Terra glanced over his shoulder at her, "you once asked me if I thought less of you for killing Casper. Do you think less of me for killing Kraig?"

"No. He would have haunted us for the rest of our lives. It wasn't enough that he escaped Hornview with wealth from all that stolen Rock Blood, he couldn't resist trying to kill us again. He hated you, Terra, because you're everything he could never be—decent, respected, and one of the fastest, most powerful Horsemen around."

"All that speed and power only means something to me because I can protect you with it. As I've always said, Inez, you're my heart."

"And you're mine." She kissed his neck. "I have something to tell you. I didn't want to let you know until we left the tropics because I didn't think you'd let me on those last couple of Gatherings, and you probably would have been right. I promise, however, not to do anything foolish until about seven months from now — or will it be longer? I'm not sure if Horsemen babies take more time."

"Baby?" He smiled at her, his ears wiggling and eyes gleaming as he stopped. "Get off my back and into my arms, woman!"

Grinning, Inez slipped from him. He swept her into his arms and covered her mouth with a long, tender kiss. When it broke, his brow furrowed. "You went on those damn Gatherings with our baby in you? Are you crazy? And then Kraig dropped you from the Gods know what height! Bad flights won't kill me, but you will. From now on no more — "

Inez interrupted him with a kiss. She whispered against his lips, "Please shut up, Terra. I will be careful from now on. Do you hope it's a boy?"

"I don't care what it is." He squeezed her tighter, brushing his lips across her forehead. "It'll be ours."

"I hope it doesn't have my mouth," she said as he continued toward their cottage, her body still snug against his chest.

"I hope it doesn't have my nose — unless it's a male and he needs good breathing for long flights."

"I hope it has your eyes."

"And your hair."

And so the conversation continued over the crest of the hill toward home.

The End

Enjoy this excerpt from
Captive Stallion
Horsemen

Moor had never dropped or harmed a rider in his life, even during the worst of journeys.

The flight went better than expected until the last of the Spikelands faded in the distance, leaving only the endless stretch of sea. A sharp turn to keep himself righted against a powerful gust of wind drew a fresh blood flow from Moor's injured arm. He gasped with pain and squeezed his free hand to the arm. Jonis tore off part of a blanket in the saddle pack and helped Moor bind the injury again—a difficult procedure while in midair. Moments later, he'd bled through the bandage. Moor felt light-headed from blood loss. Sweat soaked his coat. His lungs felt ready to explode from gasping in the frigid air.

Gods, it's too far to go. His heart pounded, skipping beats as he struggled to keep himself on an even flight pattern.

"I'm unloading the cargo," Jonis called to him.

Unable to expend the energy to reply, Moor continued flying. Through blurry eyes, he thought he saw the water looming close, the dark, deadly reeds stretching toward his churning equine legs.

"Pull up. Pull up," Jonis bellowed. "We're too close to the ocean!"

Moor did his best to fly upward against the wind. His breath rasped and he felt Jonis press closer to his man-torso as he struggled to unfasten the saddle. They'd risked their lives to gather the Rock Blood humans desperately needed and the saddle was one of his best, but at that moment Moor didn't care about either. Survival was foremost in his mind. Survival and agony. His lungs and muscles were on fire and the loss of blood had weakened him so much he felt on the verge of blacking out. Suddenly the weight of the saddle was gone and he managed a deep breath. He forced his wings and legs upward. Was he succeeding in his ascent?

"Moor," a voice bellowed to his left.

He forced himself to focus on Terra. Another Horseman dropped near his right, holding a support strap.

Terra loomed close, his rider reaching for Jonis. Was the younger Horseman crazy? How could he possibly fly the rest of the way home with two riders and cargo? Such a flight could kill a Carrier. Still, Terra was powerful and well trained. He might be able to handle it. Moor himself had undergone flights with unusually heavy loads. Just by taking his rider, Terra was probably saving his life as well as Jonis's. Moor knew he had the strength to fly for himself, though he would have sank to his death before ever unloading a rider.

With the burden of his rider gone, Moor's head cleared and his breathing became easier. He felt something graze his belly. The Horseman to his left had thrown the support line underneath Moor's equine body and another Carrier caught it from the other side. The two smaller Horsemen rose over his head. One of them held both ends of the strap. If Moor felt the need, he could lean on the strap to rest during the flight home while the Carrier above helped support him.

Knowing he had assistance, that the others in his party were willing to risk their lives to help him and Jonis, fueled his strength. He beat his wings harder and after a moment rose to a safe distance above the sea.

Not once did he lean into the support strap, unwilling to overburden the Carrier above him unless absolutely forced to. Several times the other members of the party flew in to offer help. Only one Carrier refused to assist. Kraig flew ahead, only glancing back to fire looks of rage and jealousy at Terra who flew just ahead of Moor, his motions remarkably steady for a Horseman carrying too much weight. As the journey progressed, Moor noted through his own discomfort, that Terra flew more slowly than usual. The wind blew lather from his black equine coat, revealing the toll taken on his overburdened body. Moor felt overwhelmed with gratitude for his friend and rage toward Kraig. The redhead was also a large Carrier, well able to share the burden of the second rider for at least part of the journey. Terra was a true Fighting Carrier, but Moor wondered how Kraig had even earned a position in the elite force. It took more than speed and power to be a Fighting Carrier. It took loyalty, courage, and heart, qualities Kraig didn't have.

By the end of the journey, Moor had lost so much blood he was almost unconscious in flight. His wings beat and legs churned without thought. As torch lights from the Running Way near the village square shone like fuzzy dots in the distance, Moor wondered if the vision of home wasn't some trick of his dying mind.

His crash landing proved that he was still very much alive. His knees scraped the packed dirt ground and his equine body slammed hard on its side. What wind he had left was knocked out of him. Unable to do more than gasp and wheeze, he lay still until he felt gentle arms slip around him. Tender, frantic hands probed his bloodied torso. As his eyes focused on Inez, he felt awash with relief. His foster daughter looked terrified as she searched for his wound.

"Arm," he grunted in pain.

Suddenly another pair of small hands found the wound. These hands were sure and deft as they sliced away the bloodied piece of blanket and began cleansing the injury.

His eyes focused on Susana. Though young, she was highly skilled. Blond hair fell across her delicate face as she worked on his arm. He thought she said something about cauterizing the wound, but he was nearly unconscious again. The burning of his flesh roused him slightly and he groaned.

Inez asked what happened to Moor's rider. Someone told her Terra had flown him in. Moments later, she was gone, probably to see to her husband. In the back of his mind, Moor hoped Terra hadn't damaged himself by making such an arduous flight carrying two men and cargo.

"You'll be all right," Susana told him in a soothing voice. Her hand gently gripped his shoulder. "Linn and a few others have gone for some buckets of water to cool you down, then you can get back to the longhouse and rest."

About the author:

A lifelong fan of action and romance, Kate Hill likes heroes with a touch of something wicked and wild. Her short fiction and poetry have appeared in publications both on and off the Internet. When she's not working on her books, Kate enjoys dancing, martial arts, and researching vampires and Viking history

Kate welcomes mail from readers. You can write to her c/o Ellora's Cave Publishing at 1337 Commerce Drive, Suite 13, Stow OH 44224.

Why an electronic book?

We live in the Information Age — an exciting time in the history of human civilization in which technology rules supreme and continues to progress in leaps and bounds every minute of every hour of every day. For a multitude of reasons, more and more avid literary fans are opting to purchase e-books instead of paperbacks. The question to those not yet initiated to the world of electronic reading is simply: *why?*

1. *Price.* An electronic title at Ellora's Cave Publishing runs anywhere from 40-75% less than the cover price of the <u>exact same title</u> in paperback format. Why? Cold mathematics. It is less expensive to publish an e-book than it is to publish a paperback, so the savings are passed along to the consumer.

2. *Space.* Running out of room to house your paperback books? That is one worry you will never have with electronic novels. For a low one-time cost, you can purchase a handheld computer designed specifically for e-reading purposes. Many e-readers are larger than the average handheld, giving you plenty of screen room. Better yet, hundreds of titles can be stored within your new library — a single microchip. (Please note that Ellora's Cave does not endorse any specific brands. You can check our website at www.ellorascave.com for customer recommendations we make available to new consumers.)

3. *Mobility*. Because your new library now consists of only a microchip, your entire cache of books can be taken with you wherever you go.

4. *Personal preferences are accounted for*. Are the words you are currently reading too small? Too large? Too...ANNOYING? Paperback books cannot be modified according to personal preferences, but e-books can.

5. *Innovation*. The way you read a book is not the only advancement the Information Age has gifted the literary community with. There is also the factor of what you can read. Ellora's Cave Publishing will be introducing a new line of interactive titles that are available in e-book format only.

6. *Instant gratification.* Is it the middle of the night and all the bookstores are closed? Are you tired of waiting days—sometimes weeks—for online and offline bookstores to ship the novels you bought? Ellora's Cave Publishing sells instantaneous downloads 24 hours a day, 7 days a week, 365 days a year. Our e-book delivery system is 100% automated, meaning your order is filled as soon as you pay for it.

Those are a few of the top reasons why electronic novels are displacing paperbacks for many an avid reader. As always, Ellora's Cave Publishing welcomes your questions and comments. We invite you to email us at service@ellorascave.com or write to us directly at: 1337 Commerce Drive, Suite 13, Stow OH 44224.

NEED A MORE EXCITING
WAY TO PLAN YOUR DAY?

ELLORA'S
CAVEMEN

2006 CALENDAR

COMING THIS FALL

The
ELLORA'S CAVE
Library

Stay up to date with Ellora's Cave Titles
in Print with our Quarterly Catalog.

To recieve a catalog,
send an email with your name
and mailing address to:

CATALOG@ELLORASCAVE.COM

or send a letter or postcard
with your mailing address to:
Catalog Request
c/o Ellora's Cave Publishing, Inc.
1337 Commerce Drive #13
Stow, OH 44224

Lady Jaided

The premier magazine for today's sensual woman

Lady Jaided magazine is devoted to exploring the sexuality and sensuality of women. While there are many similarities between the sexual experiences of men and women, there are just as many if not more differences. Our focus is on the female experience and on giving voice and credence to it. Lady Jaided will include everything from trends, politics, science and history to gossip, humor and celebrity interviews, but our focus will remain on female sexuality and sensuality.

A Sneak Peek at Upcoming Stories

Clan of the Cave Woman
Women's sexuality throughout history.

The Sarandon Syndrome
What's behind the attraction between older women and younger men.

The Last Taboo
Why some women – even feminists – have bondage fantasies

Girls' Eyes for Queer Guys
An in-depth look at the attraction between straight women and gay men

Available Spring 2005

www.LadyJaided.com

Discover for yourself why readers can't get enough of the multiple award-winning publisher Ellora's Cave. Whether you prefer e-books or paperbacks, be sure to visit EC on the web at www.ellorascave.com for an erotic reading experience that will leave you breathless.

www.ellorascave.com